If You But Knew

April Bennett

To Wray Ann—
Happy reading!
April
2015

If You But Knew

ISBN-13: 978-1-511-73616-9
ISBN-10: 1-511-73616-X

Cover design by Adrienne Pearson

For soulmates and kindred spirits.
May we each find our own.

And for Michael, without whom
life would be an utter bore.

Chapter 1

Jenny stood in the doorway, smiling at the scene before her. Her garden was beginning to embrace spring, and the lilacs were coming into bud. Lilacs had always been at the top of her list of favorite flowers. To Jenny, lilacs meant new beginnings. Sometimes it still took her by surprise that "She of the Black Thumb" had become the owner of a real, honest-to-goodness English cottage-style garden. In a few short weeks the garden would be glorious, the greens lush and deep, and a riot of colorful blooms surrounding her sweet bungalow. It was a blessing that the previous owners had recommended the gardener they'd used. Jenny would have turned the lovely garden into a weed-choked mess before the summer was over last year. She could never remember when or how much to water things, but Andrew was magic with plants.

She rummaged in her bag for the keys and as she locked the door, Jenny thought back over the past three years. When David had died so suddenly, Jenny thought she might die too. They were supposed to live happily ever after, everyone had said so! She'd even believed that they'd been soulmates, destined for each other and a long, full life. It wasn't fair that he had been taken away. Forty-somethings don't have strokes – and they certainly don't die. But he had, and she hadn't, and eventually Jenny peeked out of the shell she'd built around herself. She'd needed to start fresh, where she could be her own person, where she didn't think of him at every turn. She'd been here in her new home almost a year now, a year of finding herself, of remaking herself. She was finally beginning to feel normal. Even (dared she say it?) happy.

"Good morning, Mrs. M.!" Andrew called out cheerfully. He was just letting himself into the garden as Jenny turned to go. "Off to work already?"

"Yep. Early staff meeting. You know, big important stuff at the library! And Andrew, I told you to call me Jenny. You aren't 12 anymore; having adults call me "Mrs." makes me feel old!" Jenny smiled and shook her head. Andrew had been friends with her sons, Josh and Ryan, all through school, although they'd lost touch in college. He had always been thoroughly polite, and always addressed her as Mrs. Martin or Mrs. M. When she'd hired him last year, she'd insisted he call her Jenny, though he'd respectfully refused. It was endearing, really. He was unfailingly courteous, and he was a hard worker. Jenny knew she could count on him to be there when he said he would, even though she'd seen him working for many of her neighbors, too. She didn't know how he kept his schedule straight, but she appreciated his efforts, nonetheless.

"Oh, could you please look at the back storm door? The wind caught it the other day, and I think the spring is messed up. I don't know if it can be fixed, but if anyone can do it, it's you!"

Andrew ran his fingers through his short-cropped hair and grinned. "Sure thing! Anything for my favorite boss!"

"Aww, I'm sure you say that to all the ladies; and we all love it! Never change a thing, Andrew!" Jenny sauntered off to work with a smile on her face and thought that today would be a very good day.

Andrew watched her leave, his smile fading. She really had no idea that he was half in love with her, did she? Hell, he'd been half in love with her for as long as he could remember. From the time he'd started noticing girls, really. When she hired him last year, all those latent feelings had come welling up. She was just as beautiful as she had been ten years ago, her long dark hair pulled away from her face as always, emphasizing her smile and expressive grey-green eyes. There was a lingering sadness in those eyes that made his heart ache for her.

She treated him as an equal now, an adult. Which, of course, he was, but sometimes he still felt a little like the skinny, horny, tongue-tied teenager he'd been. He couldn't even imagine what Josh would do if he found out. Probably beat him to a bloody pulp. That's what he would do, if his buddy put the moves on his mom! Andrew gave himself a mental shake and went to work. There were things to get done today, no time for wishful thinking!

Yet the memory of Jenny's smiling face beguiled him all day. Did he imagine that she looked more vibrant lately? The sadness was melting away like the last winter's snow, and in its place, he could see optimism. Something was different, and it made her even more beautiful.

"Karen, get your bag, we're going to lunch. My treat." Jenny barged into the office with barely a knock. It was hard to stand on ceremony with one's oldest and best friend since grade school.

"Well, aren't you the chipper one? What are we celebrating?"

"Don't you think it's a good day today? It's just a good day." With a smile she suggested they get a sandwich from the deli down the street and sit in the park for their lunch hour. Karen went along for the ride. While Jenny was good-natured and sunny, this was new. Something was different, and Karen couldn't wait to find out why.

"Cough it up, Sister. This is an extra special good mood. What's got you all frisky?"

"I don't know, honestly! It's just, spring is in the air and I feel…different. A good different. It must be May Day magic."

"Well, I can tell. You are positively sparkling today. Whatever it is, I like it! Not new shoes, or a new dress?" *Or a new man?* Karen kept that question to herself, but it certainly made her wonder. She hadn't seen sweet little Jenny sparkle like this since, well, since before David had died. The light had gone out of her eyes then, and Karen hadn't been sure she'd ever see it again. Whatever, or *whomever*, had happened, Karen was thrilled!

"Neither." Jenny replied. "I haven't been shopping lately, although I think it's time for new sandals and sundresses. Maybe this weekend?" Jenny left the invitation up in the air and laughed in anticipation of the trip. She considered herself a mostly practical person, but she definitely had a weakness for shoes and skirts. She'd always been a bit of a girly-girl, and as the only woman in a household of men, Karen had been her go-to shopping partner. David didn't care about the dresses she so loved, much less the clothes he wore, as long as they were clean.

Jenny grew serious for a moment, trying to find the words to explain to her friend what, precisely, was different. Karen was right. She felt lighter and free. She just had to figure out how to describe exactly what she was feeling in a way that made sense.

"Karen, have you ever just woken up one morning and felt that something was going to happen? You weren't sure what, but *something*? I don't know if I should call it a premonition; it's not that, but something's coming, even the air is different. Oh, I'm not making sense. I don't know how to explain it. Nothing has changed, but…"

"I know, Sweetpea. Nothing has changed, but everything looks different, right?" Karen was subdued and thoughtful. It was time (long past time) for a change, but it had had to be Jenny's timing, not Karen's. *Looks like*

Jenny is ready for that change, she thought. Karen wanted so much for Jenny to be happy again. It made her almost tearful to think it.

"That's it exactly. I knew you'd understand. It's like David and I…it's like I've finally said goodbye, and I'm ready to start living again. I know he would want me to find a new love. But before, I felt…I felt like I was betraying our marriage to even *imagine* looking, and honestly the idea of enduring that sort of heartache again was unthinkable. This doesn't mean I'm going on a date every weekend, and maybe not even at all. No one has asked, and I haven't really looked, either!" She fiddled with the paper wrapping from her sandwich. "But I think I'm finally ready. I think…"

The silence stretched as Karen thought about how much to say, and how much to leave unsaid. She finally decided to say nothing. She only squeezed her friend's hand and smiled. Next time, she thought. *Next time we'll talk about all the men who keep asking me to set them up with my cute friend.* Karen was going to have to beat them off with a stick once they found out Jenny was available.

Jenny came home with too many bags. How she let Karen talk her into so many new things this time she'd never know. Shopping at the outlets was a dangerous endeavor with her partner in crime! At least she'd done most of her shopping on the clearance racks. Getting a beautiful bargain was one of the little joys in life. And then there was the charming yellow sundress, begging her to take it home, even though it was a bit more than she had meant to spend.

She opened the kitchen door and dropped her bags on the table, deciding there was time enough to put them away after she checked on dinner. It smelled delicious! Jenny had tossed the carrots, beef and potatoes into the crock with her favorite herb blend this morning before leaving, and had been anticipating dinner all day. Fork-tender meat and perfectly cooked veggies, simple and scrumptious. All she had left to do was warm a baguette to go with everything.

Jenny didn't use the slow cooker much after the winter, but she'd been in a pot roast kind of mood this morning. Too bad she was alone tonight; roast was a meal made for sharing. She was used to it, though, and was rather looking forward to some solitude this evening, wanting nothing more than to put her feet up and veg out in front of the television. Jenny gathered her loot and headed to her bedroom. Time for lounge pants and a hoodie.

Jenny was just pulling a tee shirt over her head when she heard the doorbell. *Well, crap.* Now that she was home and settled, she realized just how tired she was;

shopping was a great deal of fun, but her endurance wasn't what it used to be. She never could ignore a doorbell or a phone. Jenny quickly tugged on her lounge pants and yelled out, "Just a minute!"

Perhaps Andrew had been mistaken; she wasn't home after all. Just as he stepped off the porch, he heard her voice calling from the back of the house. Even though he was here for business, his heart skipped a beat. It was good to see Jenny. Mrs. Martin. *Mrs. Martin, Josh's mom, your client.* But in his mind, she was always Jenny. Her name suited her, feminine and soft, and not too fussy. Speaking of not too fussy, he could see her through the window, ambling toward the front door in an old tee shirt and some god-awful plaid pants. Where had she found those monstrosities? She still looked adorable. The ensemble drifted over her curves, hinting at a lush figure, but not quite revealing it.

As she neared the door, she could see Andrew on the porch. *Just great,* she thought. *I probably should at least have put on jeans – something more presentable than…* She glanced down at her threadbare pajamas. *Dear Lord.* At least she still had her hair and makeup done. She opened up the door with a self-conscious smile.

"Hey, there, what can I do for you?"

"Hi, Mrs. Martin. I'm sorry to bother you; I should have just called, but I was walking by, and, well, I wanted to ask if it's okay with you if we switch around our weekly schedule a bit. I have some new clients this summer who want me in the mornings, and I thought you probably wouldn't mind switching to an evening. Is that okay with you?"

"Sure, Andrew, of course it's okay. You can come anytime you want, so long as my petunias don't die!" She laughed. It was silly to have him come over at all, really, but she was genuinely afraid she'd kill her beautiful garden, and it was nice to have a caretaker for it. Extravagant, but nice. "Would Tuesdays and Fridays be a good place to start? And, maybe one day, I can shadow you. I really should learn to take care of this myself. Just show me what not to weed out, how often to water things, and how and when to prune. You know, everything I need to know to put you out of a job!"

"Aw, Mrs. M., I'm not sure I can do that. Put myself out of a job? But, well, I suppose..." He gestured to include the whole garden behind him. "You think you can learn all this in one summer?" He made the teasing remark before he realized it was out of his mouth.

Jenny laughed out loud. "Of course! If you can do it, surely I can!" The gleam in her eye was positively devious.

Andrew stood there, momentarily speechless, and then chuckled with her. Good grief, she'd zinged him! "Touché, Mrs. M. Touché."

She suddenly found that she wasn't so tired anymore; she felt oddly invigorated. Jenny realized they were still standing in the doorway. *How rude of you not to invite him in! What is wrong with you, Jenny?*

"Oh, goodness! Please, come in and sit for a minute. Are you still working? Surely not! It's past dinner time." Jenny closed the door as Andrew walked in and led him to the sofa. She sat in the corner, pulling her legs underneath her and propping her elbows on her knees, leaning expectantly forward as she waited for his response. Andrew had no choice but to follow, carefully choosing the recliner beside her, rather than the sofa cushion next to her.

"Actually, yeah. I work a lot, even on weekends. Gotta work while the weather's good, you know. I get handyman calls at all hours. I think my name and number get passed around at the senior center. It's not a bad thing, though. Word of mouth is the best advertising there is, and if my clients are happy, then I'm happy."

"Andrew, that's great! And very true. So, tell me. How'd you ever get started as a landscaper slash handyman anyway? I thought you were going to go to school for computer-something? I guess I never thought to ask before." Jenny realized that she really knew almost nothing about Andrew. She'd known him as a boy, as much as she'd known any of the kids' friends, but she didn't know the young man he'd become. Jenny was curious. She remembered overhearing him once say that he wanted to be a programmer, and was going to live in the city – anywhere but this tiny Ohio town. It was much too provincial for his tastes.

"It's funny," Andrew said. "I'm not doing what I thought I'd be doing, but I guess life's like that. What's that saying? Life's what happens when we're busy making plans.

I came home after graduation. Just for the summer, you know, while I was still applying for the hundred dream jobs I was *immensely* qualified for as a new graduate with no experience." He offered a self-deprecating laugh as he continued, "Well, while I was home, my grandpa got sick. So I moved in with the grandparents, and helped them every day with, well, with whatever. Daily chores, fixing up the house, anything Gramps would have done. And somehow, I found myself helping at their friends' houses, too. Just doing whatever needed to be done. More and more, the favors became jobs." He thought about that first year and how readily he'd slid into the role of handyman.

"I never asked, not at first, but people have their pride, and they would pay me anyway. It was rude not to accept, and they wouldn't let me. You try saying no to a bossy grandmother!" He smiled at the memories. "So, I spent less time on my resume and applications, and more time weeding and watering gardens, planting the petunias and hostas, fixing toilets and doors and building wheelchair ramps. Before I knew it, I was working full time as a handyman."

Jenny looked at him with a new respect. How many kids his age would have helped out their grandparents like that? Not many, she would guess. And then to stick around and make a business opportunity of it. Interesting, to say the least.

"When I finally got a job in my field, it turns out it was right under my nose. A client's son needed a web designer and a networking guy, and he hired me based on his dad's glowing recommendation of my work ethic. It's the weirdest thing. Would you believe Mark runs a multi-million dollar company from a little warehouse just outside of town? I spent all of college being 'anywhere but here,' looking forward to getting out of Alandale and moving to Chicago or some other big urban 'happening town,' and yet, here I am, doing what I was meant to do – I think. I get to keep my hand in with the computers, on my own schedule, and I get to work for some truly amazing people. You should hear some of the stories these old men have to tell. They have lived through so much. It's humbling." Andrew grew quiet, thinking back.

He didn't often think about how he'd ended up here, but if he hadn't stayed, well, life was a funny thing.

She ventured a question, hoping she wasn't being insensitive. "And, your Gramps? Is he still around?"

His face softened and his eyes held a sadness she recognized all too well. "Nah… He died. Gram, too. I guess she didn't much like being here without him. But, you know. It was a while ago – it's fine now." He was quick to reassure her when he saw how her face fell at his answer. It was a sad thing, but part of life. She knew that as well as anyone. He didn't want Jenny to be upset, so he changed the subject with the first question he could think of. "So, how are things at the library? Anything new?"

She smiled. "Are you kidding me? Things are always new and exciting at the library! We have a new collection of murder-mysteries on the Features table, with new books coming in every week. We also are updating our dinosaur computers this summer. I'll bring you in for the full tour when everything is set." She giggled, but quickly stifled the girlish sound. *Did that come from me? Since when do I giggle?* Jenny decided it must be whatever was new in the air lately.

"Um…I know this is a little strange, but would you like to stay for dinner? I made a whole pot roast just for myself, and it would be nice to share it with someone. I was going to watch a movie while I ate, but I mean, if you don't have somewhere to be, or if you haven't already eaten. Oh heavens. Never mind! Forget I said anything!" She felt immediately disconcerted, both by her desire to have him stay, and her awkwardly worded invitation. And a thought suddenly occurred to her. *Oh no! He's going to think I'm hitting on him!*

"Oh, Mrs. M., I really can't today. But thank you for asking." *What the hell are you doing? The woman of your dreams just asked you to stay for dinner!* Andrew hoped he sounded polite and calm. On the inside, he was screaming at himself for turning her down.

"No worries! It was a long shot, and crazy of me to ask." She was kicking herself for doing so. What was she thinking?

"Well, it smells delicious. I remember your cooking from school days. I wouldn't miss it if I didn't have somewhere to be." *Somewhere to be? Andrew, you are a complete idiot. And seriously, do you really have to remind her that she used to feed you when you were a kid? Way to go…*

"Maybe another time, then." Jenny said. "Have a good night." She walked him to the door and locked it behind him. Well, dinner alone it would be. Half an hour ago, the thought didn't bother her at all. Now, though, it seemed so depressing.

Chapter 2

Jenny was roused from sleep by the most delicious dream. Though she couldn't quite see a face, she could feel hands and lips caressing her body. Neck and shoulder and breast and waist. It was delightful. And erotic. A part of her that had vanished with the death of her husband had not only reappeared, but was ferociously demanding attention. This was the spring of re-awakening, that's for sure. It was impossible to ignore, and further, she didn't want to. Jenny could almost feel the weight of a lover at her side, the heat of his body warming hers. He smelled of spicy cologne, but underneath was a scent that was his alone. Reluctantly opening her eyes, Jenny hoped for a dream-turned-reality, but knew her bed would be empty, and she would be going to work frustrated again. *Damn, it's going to be a very long day. It's definitely time for a man in my life.*

"Good morning, Andrew! How are you today?" Jenny had just closed the kitchen door behind her when Andrew sauntered up from the driveway. She was pleasantly surprised to see him, since he'd just talked to her about changing days.

"Doin' great, Mrs. Martin." He smiled and stopped next to her for a moment. He ran his fingers nervously over his short blond hair. He hadn't expected to see her this morning. "I know we just discussed a switch-up, but I left a few things here last time I worked, thinking I'd be here first today. Shoulda picked them up the other day, but I completely forgot."

Of course he'd forgotten. He'd been busy beating himself up for turning down a hot meal, even though he was just going to meet the guys for a beer. He should have stood them up.

"It's quite all right. As a matter of fact, it's perfect! I made stew out of the remaining roast. Well, most of it, actually. And I was hoping you'd take some off my hands. I'm sure you could eat half of it in one sitting, if I remember correctly. Maybe for lunch today?" She smiled at the memory of the boys and their friends sitting down to demolish in minutes meals that had taken her an hour to prepare. Boys – and men – sure did eat a lot. And if she had to guess, Andrew didn't get too many home-cooked meals. Single men usually didn't.

"Uh...yes, yeah, sure! I would love it. Thank you so much."

"You're welcome." She let them both back into the kitchen, and rummaged for a cooler to put the stew container in. "Just a second – I know I have one in here somewhere. Where is that cooler thingy? I don't use it much; Karen and I go out a lot for lunch. It's one of our indulgences. Ah, here it is!" As she bent to search the lower cabinets Andrew had a delightful view of her backside, but the moment was cut all too short when Jenny suddenly popped up with the small cooler in her hand as though it were a prize. It was a matter of moments to corral everything and hand it over. "Now, heat it in a real bowl for just a couple minutes and stir it half-way through. Ugh, what am I saying? Of course you know how to use a microwave! And there are ice blocks to keep it cold. I don't imagine you'll have time to go home before lunch. Do you even eat lunch at home? I never thought about that. I don't even know where you live. But you walk everywhere, so you must live close. Well, I won't keep you. Have a good day, and I'll see you later! I need to get myself to work, too!" Jenny was off to the library before he had a chance to thank her again.

Andrew didn't remember her being such a chatterbox. Hopefully she hadn't said anything too important. He'd tried to follow Jenny's rambling, but his eyes and mind were full of the sight of her luscious derriere. He smiled as she walked away, still admiring the view.

"I brought your bowl back. Cooler and ice blocks, too. I can't thank you enough for lunch. I don't get too many home-cooked meals lately. Since the parents moved to Florida, I've been pretty deprived! There's only Mrs. P. to take care of me, and I try not to wear out my welcome there." He laughed and patted his non-existent belly. He never felt deprived. His own brand of cooking was good enough.

"Oh, Sweetie, you stop in anytime for real food. I enjoy cooking, but with only myself to feed, I don't do much of it anymore. It's pretty sad that half the time I have a bowl of cereal for dinner as well as for breakfast! Grown women are supposed to eat better than that!" She laughed at her own lack of real home cooking. She ate like a bachelor, too, sometimes. Maybe that was why she'd fixed that big roast the other day, even knowing that she wouldn't eat most of it.

"Aw, shucks, Mrs. Martin. I would hate to impose." Always so polite. But he liked that she'd asked, and she knew it. The twinkle in his blue eyes gave him away. Maybe he was as lonely as she was for family and company sometimes.

"Oh no, it's not imposing at all, or I wouldn't have asked. Tell you what. You come on in after you finish up on Tuesdays, and we'll have a real meal together. No cereal, no peanut butter sandwiches. But don't think I'm going to do all the cooking! I have a grill, and you can use it. Men still love to cook with fire, right?" she smiled. David had loved grilling, and he'd taught both boys to love it, too. Surely this boy would know how to grill a great burger. If not, she'd teach him. Cooking was a necessary skill.

He chuckled and replied, "Men still love cooking with fire, Mrs. M., and I'm no exception. Thanks for the invite. You're just the nicest lady, you know? You always were the best mom, after my own, of course!"

Great. The best mom…when I want her to be anything but *my mother!* Andrew didn't know where these gems kept coming from. Maybe it was the long-standing habit of trying to keep a proper distance from her, but he needed to work harder on keeping them to himself. She might not mind; it seemed she'd pretty much adopted the role of surrogate mom without thinking about it. But *he* minded. If he ever wanted her to see him as an attractive, eligible male, he needed to keep his mouth shut. He wanted to figure out what made her tick. Jenny might be everything he admired in a woman, but he had no idea what she found appealing in a man. He thought back to what he remembered of Mr. Martin. Andrew remembered him as a big bear of a man, both in appearance and in personality. He was a little gruff at times, but usually friendly. And he liked a good joke. One of the things Andrew liked best about the Martin house was that it was always full of laughter. Well, he would either figure out what Jenny wanted or he wouldn't. Sharing dinner would help.

"I didn't know what you'd want for dinner, but I can't think of anyone who doesn't like pasta, so I made spaghetti. Sound good?" She wanted to please – she always wanted to please – and tonight was no exception.

"I'll eat anything. I'm starving today." Andrew was famished. He'd had an emergency call to the warehouse and had ended up working through lunch to get the network back online. Businesses nowadays could barely function without an internet connection.

"Oh, good. I made lots! Figured you could take home whatever leftovers there might be." She giggled, "Once a mom, always a mom, I guess. Now, wash up and tell me what you want to drink, then tell me about your day."

"Alrighty. Milk please. Are you sure I can't do anything to help?" Jenny waved him away, so he quickly washed and sat down, grateful to finally rest after the day's hard labor. "My day was good. There were a few moments of frustration with the computer network at the warehouse, but we got everything in working order again, and then it was off to the Petersens' for the afternoon. I'm putting in new flower beds, now that Mrs. Petersen has decided where she wants them. It took her a good two months to make up her mind on it. Sweet lady, but she has the absolute worst time making any decisions. It's a good thing I have the patience of a saint!" He laughed, "And they're some of my favorite clients. They happen to live right next door to me. Mr. and Mrs. P. were good friends of my grandparents, and they kind of adopted me after Gram and Gramps died. They're more than just neighbors or clients, you know?"

"That's sweet! I'm not sure I know Mr. Petersen, but Mrs. Petersen is in the library all the time. She is lovely. And you're right, she can't make decisions. Luckily, she's read most of the large-print books in our branch, so there are fewer choices. It's lovely you have them to take care of you, and that you do the same for them."

She served up an enormous helping of spaghetti in her special meat sauce, and placed a slice of toasted baguette on the side. "Eat – eat! Between bites you can tell me about you. All my information on you is ten years out of date. Tell me *everything*." She smiled and her grey-green eyes danced as she spoke.

"Everything? That may take a while, but if you have the time, then let's get started." Andrew laughed and took a bite. His eyes closed in ecstasy as he gestured to the plate. He remembered this from high school, not that he was going to say anything about it this time! The sauce was so thick and meaty. He would do anything and everything not to screw up this sweet deal – dinner on Tuesdays with a beautiful woman.

"I'm glad you like it, Andrew." Jenny was inordinately pleased that he liked her cooking. It was silly, really. But she so rarely cooked for anyone, and it was nice to be appreciated again. She hadn't realized how much she missed it.

"Hey, when are you joining me in the yard? I thought you wanted to learn how to garden for yourself?" And he wanted to see her less than perfect and smudged with potting soil.

"Oh, yes, you're right. I did say that, didn't I? I suppose…when are you coming next? Friday? I can be ready to learn then." She was looking forward to it. She wanted to learn, and she'd have a great teacher. It would be fun!

They spent the evening talking and joking and laughing as they finished dinner and while Andrew helped her clean up the kitchen.

"What's your favorite music? I bet you listen to classical stuff, don't you, Mrs. Librarian?" Andrew threw her a teasing look as he dried the last bowl. Music in the Martin house seemed always to be whatever the boys were listening to at the time. He really had no idea what her preference was.

Jenny laughed, "Mrs. Librarian? Do I look so old and straitlaced then?" She pushed a lock of hair behind her ear and looked at him. "I do like classical, but I listen to a bit of everything." A sly smile emerged as she thought of her secret musical passion. She wondered how surprised he'd be to hear that in her youth she'd been a bit of a rocker. She'd collected all the albums she could from the hair metal bands of the Eighties. Occasionally she would play an old record on a Saturday afternoon as she did her chores or tackled a project. "Ok, Mr. Handyman, what do you like? I'll bet you're into Country & Western." She took a stab in the dark, based on his work uniform and beat up old truck.

He loved classic rock and collected old albums, particularly anything he could find by Rush. Andrew liked metal of any sort, though, new or old. He wondered if Jenny ever listened to that stuff. "I like a bit of everything, too. Mostly rock. Sometimes country, if I'm drinking. It's good stuff to drown sorrows in." He smiled at her. "You didn't really tell me what your favorite is."

"No, I didn't, did I?" The teasing smile appeared once again before she turned to hide her giggle. For some reason teasing him came so naturally.

They lingered over their conversation late into the evening, until Andrew reluctantly made the move to leave.

"Oh, heavens! It's late, isn't it! I'm sure you have an early start to your morning. Oh, Andrew, thank you for spending the evening with me."

"It was absolutely my pleasure, Mrs. M. I haven't eaten so well since, well, since you fed me beef stew last week. Thank you. For stew and for spaghetti, and for everything." Andrew didn't know what to say that didn't sound like he was talking to his mother, and he was hesitant to ask if he could come next week. It seemed too good to be true to have a standing dinner date with Jenny. *Even if she does treat me like an extra son…*

"You are so welcome. I'll see you on Friday, and you can teach me a thing or two about plants and weeds, and we'll decide what we'll have next week for dinner. You'll come?" She hoped he'd come. He was a sweet boy with an old soul. She knew he was only in his mid-twenties, but he seemed older. Jenny was surprised at how much they had in common, and how swiftly the time had passed.

Friday couldn't come quickly enough. Andrew was looking forward to his time with Jenny, much more than he ought to. He had to constantly remind himself that Mrs. Martin was a boss of sorts, and that she saw no more in their meeting than a friendly learning session. It was true, of course. There was no denying that her demeanor and her eyes showed nothing of romantic interest, and everything of motherly interest. Yet, he couldn't quite squash the hope that spending extra time with her would kindle a spark in her, that she would begin to see him not as another son, but as a…a what? A love interest, he supposed.

He'd never thought about what sort of relationship they could have, beyond that he wanted to be with her. It had always been impossible, so he'd never gone beyond daydreams of time spent together, and, though he would never admit it to anyone, he fantasized about making love to her. He tried not to. That was a rabbit hole leading straight to misery. *Wanting what you can't have… Andrew, get a grip!*

Chapter 3

Karen and Jenny were just finishing up their walk in the Reserve.

"So, have you decided when I get to set you up on your first date? I have a list a mile long of guys who want to meet you…"

"Oh, really? That's a whole lot of men!" Jenny smiled at the exaggeration, and thought yet again that perhaps she'd been a little premature to mention her intention to start dating.

"Alright, maybe not a mile, but there are quite a few. There's no time like the present. And, Sweetie, I can see it in your eyes. You want to, but you're not sure how to start. You just need to jump in and do it. It's like diving into a pool. Once you're in, the water's great and you'll have fun! Trust me, Jenny."

"Of course I trust you! But perhaps I should check in with the boys first? You know, give them a heads-up."

"Jen, you're being ridiculous. You're a grown woman, and you are not going to ask their permission to go out with someone! What century do you think this is?" Sometimes Jenny was just so old-fashioned. Karen was occasionally baffled by Jenny's need to make sure the menfolk in her life approved of her decisions. Jenny's face showed her dismay and hurt and Karen was as quick to soothe as she had been to criticize.

"Jenny, Sweetpea, are you *really* ready, or are you just feeling like you *ought* to be ready? You can grieve as long as you want, if that's truly what's bothering you. You don't have to do this. Heaven knows David was one-of-a-kind. I know what you had was special, but, Sweetie, you can't live in the past. Oh, I don't mean that the way it sounds." She stopped walking and turned to her friend, holding her hands to emphasize her point.

"I'm sorry. I really thought, after our conversation before, that you *wanted* to move ahead. I definitely see a difference in you. But if that isn't it, then I won't bug you anymore. All right?"

Jenny's eyes welled with tears. She tried to reassure her friend, as well as herself.

"No, Karen. I *am* ready for this. I said so and I meant it. I feel like I'm just waking up from a long sleep. But I want to tell the boys first. Not ask – *tell*. I don't want them to be surprised by anything. Who knows?" Jenny forced some enthusiasm into her voice. "I might fall in love this summer, and I want them to be prepared for a new man in my life and, by extension, in theirs." Jenny tried to lighten the mood. "Now, about my requirements in a new gentleman friend…" She smiled determinedly and launched into a laundry list of her ideal man's qualities.

"He must have all his teeth; I prefer a full head of hair, but that's negotiable. Reasonably fit – no big beer bellies! He must be tall and dark and handsome…" Jenny trailed off as she noticed the young man approaching them on the path.

"Well, hi, Mrs. Martin, Mrs. Wallace! How are ya?" Andrew was out for his daily run on the trails a little later than usual. He might have to make this his usual time if running into Jenny was a possibility. He slowed his pace and came to a stop in front of the ladies.

"Good morning, Andrew! We're doing quite well. You?" Jenny positively glowed. Karen found herself wondering, *is he the real reason she is hesitant? Her sparkle is unmistakable, except that she seems not to notice at all. Sweet Jenny, you can't be that naïve, can you?*

"Great! It's a gorgeous day for a run – or a walk!" He grinned at the ladies, waggling his eyebrows suggestively at Jenny, then Karen. "You come here often?"

"We're here a few days a week, you naughty boy!" Karen teased. "Call me and I'll give you my schedule." Karen was quick to flirt, and it was easy to flirt with such a handsome man. He played along nicely, and gave her his full attention with small talk before carrying on with his run. Karen watched his retreating form.

"He's steamy, don't you think? Nice legs." Karen watched carefully while Jenny formed a response.

"Karen, you're incorrigible! He's young enough to be your son!" Jenny laughed, though. "But yeah…nice legs. Runners usually have good legs, don't they?" Jenny didn't remember ever seeing him in shorts before. Probably why she'd never noticed those fine legs. She caught herself staring into the distance, remembering his muscled chest gleaming with sweat as he'd approached them at the curve in the path. Jenny shook off the image and returned to the conversation.

"Right. Well, back to my list! Tall, dark and handsome; nice eyes. I don't care what color." Jenny rambled on about what she thought she'd like while Karen thought back on their meeting with Andrew. He was neither tall nor dark, although he was definitely handsome, and of course, he had a terrific runner's body. He may have been showering Karen with attention, but

Karen couldn't help feeling that his mind was really on Jenny, and Jenny never took her eyes off him. There was a connection there, no matter that Jenny was oblivious and Andrew tried to hide it. *Hmm... He's hiding his interest in Jenny, but why?*

"So, tell me about Andrew. What sort of work does he do? Can he fix my kitchen sink? You know I've been wanting to replace that faucet, and dear Danny is never going to get around to it. I could hire Andrew – if you think..."

"Of course he can do it. Andrew does just about anything. I'm sure he can replace a leaky faucet. The only things I think he doesn't do are the more specialized electrical or plumbing jobs. But a kitchen sink is basic; he can do that! And any gardening/landscaping things too. He's a real jack-of-all-trades. Let me give you his number." Jenny fished around in her bag for her phone. She quickly scrolled to his phone number and rattled it off for Karen.

"Great, thanks! I'll call him as soon as we finish lunch." Karen was disappointed. She'd thought Jenny might have more to say. She certainly liked looking at him whenever they'd run into him at the Reserve, and she had noticed they ran into him a lot the last few weeks. They'd only stopped to exchange pleasantries a couple times, but there was something. She knew she wasn't imagining things. Andrew was definitely hoping Jenny would notice him, and Jenny was stubbornly, crazily, not noticing.

"Lovely!" Jenny answered. "You'll like him; he's good. He's such a hard worker, too. Do you know he's pretty much on call all the time? Andrew started out working for his grandparents, and for their friends, and his business just grew from there. Primarily older folks who can't do what they used to for themselves. He always says to call anytime, and he actually means it! And never charges outrageous fees for late calls. He is such a sweet boy. I am sure his parents are proud he turned out so well." Jenny sounded so motherly! Karen stared hard at her friend, trying to figure out if she really meant what she'd just said. Obviously she meant the compliments, but *sweet boy?* How could she not have noticed that there was almost nothing boyish about Andrew? He was all grown up, there was no question. Time to start planting some seeds of interest. If Jenny didn't see it, it was high time she did.

"Sweet boy? Jenny, that sweet *boy* is no boy at all! He's all man, and he is one hot tamale. How can you not see this? I tell you what, if I had that eye candy in my sight all the time, I don't know how I'd get any sleep."

"Karen! Oh my gosh! He went to school with Josh. He's young enough to be my son, and I am not interested in looking at him that way." The fact that she caught herself looking occasionally was just embarrassing. "He's…I'm sure he sees me as nothing more than a schoolmate's mom. And I see him as, well, someone who works for me. I'm sure there are some ethics somewhere that say I shouldn't ogle him." Karen shouldn't suggest such things! It seemed wrong somehow. Just…*wrong*. Even if sometimes she felt drawn to him like moth to flame, it was nothing. It *had* to be nothing.

"Jenny, I hate to tell you this, but there's *nothing* wrong with looking. He is extremely handsome. And he is *not* your son, so ogle away! I am positive he doesn't mind. Men love to be ogled. It strokes their egos."

"When are we going to meet the girl?"

Andrew almost spit out his coffee. Sometimes Mrs. Petersen said the darnedest things.

"I'm sorry. What girl?" Mrs. Petersen was observant, a trait Andrew often forgot.

"Don't think I haven't noticed that you don't come round much begging for dinner. Who's the girl? Someone's been feeding you, and girls feed boys to show they care. So…?"

"Oh, that girl." Andrew had no clue how to explain Jenny, and didn't even want to try. "We're just friends, Mrs. P. Keeping each other company is all. If there's anything more, I promise you'll be one of the first to know." Andrew wished more than anything that there would someday be more, but it looked increasingly as though it was only a pipe dream. He and Jenny spent hours together every week, he was more comfortable with her than with anyone, yet it was no more than friendship. Something deep and real, but only friendship.

"Alrighty then. As long as you're eating well. I don't want to see any more bones on you." Once a grandmother, always a grandmother, it seemed.

"Yes, ma'am. I promise to eat more and put on a few pounds. If I can. How 'bout I pester you for dinner tomorrow?"

"Tomorrow would be fine, you rascal. We love having you around anytime, and well you know it. 5:30? And a game of Scrabble afterward. Mr. P. never lets me play unless you're here. Doesn't like getting whooped alone, I guess." Mrs. Petersen tossed a smug grin at Andrew, anticipating a rout of a win at their expense.

Andrew chuckled and gave Mrs. Petersen a quick hug before leaving for the day. He was lucky to have the Petersens in his life. And Mrs. Petersen and Jenny to care for him. *As if I can't take care of myself…*

Chapter 4

Jenny came home to the sight of a very busy Andrew stringing lights over and around the pergola. Tomorrow she would be celebrating her one-year anniversary in this house, and the patio was a perfect place for dinner. Her gaze swept over the table he'd moved from the storage shed and the new pots full of gorgeous blooms. Had he moved them from the front garden? She hoped so, dreading the thought of how much those might have cost, but they added a lovely touch nonetheless.

"Oh, Andrew it looks lovely already! Thank you so much for your help! I just hate nagging Josh to come over here all the time. He seems so much busier lately." She gave a self-deprecating laugh. "Of course, I'm going to put myself in the poorhouse paying for all the extra work, but you're worth every penny. I honestly don't know what I'd do without you."

"Oh, geez, don't worry about this. It's on me this time. I'm glad to help. Now, let me know if you need anything at all tomorrow. Such an important event requires a perfect setting."

"You've done so much. Are you sure you won't join us? Josh would love to see you again." She really wanted him to say yes. A year ago, she gave him about as much thought as she gave the bagger at the market. He was just always there to do his job. But since they'd begun having dinner and getting to know one another, her awareness of him had changed. It disconcerted her.

"Oh, thank you, but I can't. Really. I'm spending tomorrow evening with the Petersens. I haven't spent any time with them the last few weeks, and I need to. Besides, this should be a family affair. Josh and Ryan will enjoy having their mom all to themselves for dinner."

"Oh, well, then." Jenny covered over her disappointment with a smile, and swept her gaze over the pergola.

"That should do it. I've gotta get over to the Newmans. Fixing their washer – again. I don't know why they just don't buy a new one. With what they've paid me to fix it, I think they could have bought the top-of-the-line. But the Mrs. just won't budge. She loves that thing." He rolled his eyes and waved his goodbye. Jenny laughed with him and waved back. Poor, put-upon Andrew. Though she was quite certain that despite his complaint, he loved his job and loved helping people.

Jenny put away the groceries, and mentally ran through her list of things to do today. At the top of the list was preparing for tomorrow night's dinner: washing the linens and rinsing the china, marinating the chicken… Oh, what else? She knew she was forgetting something, but it would come to her. It always did.

Jenny slept late the next day. It was unusual for her, but a welcome change. The sun was streaming through the crack in the curtain – it must be at least nine o'clock. Time to get a move on! Dinner was tonight, and she was so eager. She hadn't seen Ryan since Easter. He lived too far away and was too busy with work to come much more than that. It made her sad sometimes, but at least he was gainfully employed. She couldn't be happier that he was working for a company he liked in a job he loved, even if it meant she rarely saw him.

Oh, heavens! If it was nine o'clock, Karen would be over any minute with coffee and pastries! They were forgoing their usual leisurely breakfast for a quick bite and shopping. Karen insisted that Jenny have a new dress for tonight's dinner. Really, it wasn't that big of a deal. She could wear the yellow one she'd bought last time. But a new dress sounded lovely. One couldn't have too many dresses, after all, Jenny mused. She hopped up and showered as quickly as she could, throwing her long chestnut hair into a ponytail and swiping on mascara and lip gloss. The rest would have to wait until tonight.

Early in the evening, Jenny remembered what she'd forgotten. Just as she was stepping into the shower for the second time that day, it hit her. *Dessert*. How could she forget dessert? She turned off the water and grabbed the phone. It was no use calling the boys, but she'd try Karen. Hopefully she'd have time to stop at the store and pick something up. Strawberries sounded good, with a bit of fresh cream. They were right in season, too, so they'd be delicious! Karen's phone went straight to voicemail. *Great*.

A knock at the kitchen door and a masculine voice calling "Halloo" distracted her from this momentary setback. She knew that voice! *Dilemma solved!* Jenny padded into the kitchen with her best persuasive smile.

"Andrew, I need to ask an enormous favor."

"Yeah? Whatcha need?" He was fiddling with the storm door again, trying to get it to catch without pulling it in. He turned around and found himself rooted to the floor where he stood.

"I forgot about dessert for tonight. Can I beg you to run to the grocery and pick up a couple pints of strawberries and a pint of whipping cream? Please? I don't have time, and Karen's not answering her phone. Let me just get some money from my purse." Andrew slowly nodded his assent, and Jenny quickly fished through the bag on the table, pulled out a twenty and handed him the bill. She beamed up at him, "Thank you so much! When you get back, just let yourself in and stick it all in the fridge. You are a doll! I have to go get ready! Thank you, Sweetie!" She tossed the last over her shoulder and went back to her shower.

Andrew was dumbstruck. Did she realize that she'd been talking to him wearing only her robe? Or that the vee of the neck perfectly framed a long sliver of golden skin that made his mouth go dry?

Two thoughts occurred to him. First, she was definitely coming out of that shell of hers. Her smile was bright and sunny and he couldn't have said no to her if he'd tried. Second, she still saw him as a boy. Or possibly a eunuch. She was completely oblivious that he was a hot-blooded male who found her extremely attractive.

If she'd realized that he was thinking of kissing every inch of that vee, and then removing her robe to kiss all the hidden inches – not to mention what they might privately do together with strawberries and whipped cream – she would have been shocked. But the notion had never occurred to her.

He turned and left to run her errand, trying hard to forget the sexy woman he'd just seen in the kitchen. She was so obviously not interested in him. The thought was depressing, to say the least.

"Dinner was divine, Jenny!" Karen was gushing. "And don't you look just lovely in a new dress? Boys, I don't suppose you noticed how lovely your mother looks tonight, did you? You might want to tell her." She winked at Ryan and smiled expectantly.

"Mom, you look great. And I love your dress. You look like a ray of sunshine!" He looked to Karen for approval, then to his brother to roll his eyes. Sure, they both knew their mom was pretty, but did they have to constantly notice and remark on it? Only Karen thought so. Aunt Karen was eccentric, he supposed.

Josh, though, noticed that something was new, something different. Maybe because he saw Mom more often, although not often enough, lately. He was about to remark on it, when Karen cleared her throat and looked tentatively at his mom. *Hmmm, something's going on.*

"Jenny, isn't there something you wanted to mention tonight?" Karen quietly encouraged her friend.

"Oh, it can wait." Her tone was nonchalant, yet she felt anything but. She was suddenly reluctant now, and she felt an unexpected ache in the region of her heart. "Ryan, tell us more about your new home; it sounds like a great place."

Ryan was only too glad to expound on his new digs – a bachelor pad shared with two friends from work, Jason and Brent. It was a gorgeous old house in a great neighborhood, and they'd completely lucked into the lease. Jenny thought it sounded marvelous, and she decided to set a date for a weekend visit before he left.

Josh interrupted Ryan's ramblings on the old house and the town. Ryan could go on forever, if the topic was himself. He needed to find out just what Karen and Mom were beating around the bush about. He was curious.

"So, Mom, what's up? You're not moving again, I hope. We've only just gotten you settled here, and I think it really suits you. You look happier." Josh finally realized what was different. Mom looked like herself again. Like she had when Dad had been around.

"Oh, Sweetheart, yes, I am happy here. I love my new home, although it's not new anymore! I've been here a whole year, which is why I invited you all to celebrate with me. You are the reason I'm here, and why I'm happy." She looked at each of them and smiled, and the tears that had been hiding in her heart began to well up in her eyes. Jenny tried tamping them down so that she could finish her thoughts.

"You boys, my menfolk, you understood when I explained my need to move a year ago, and I am going to ask you to understand again when I say that I think – I think I want to date again. I haven't met anyone, not yet, although I know Karen has a long list of prospective suitors!" She laughed a little nervously and continued.

"Your dad was my Great Love but I'm lonely without him. I always thought we'd be… But then he – oh, I am *not* going to cry! I know he wouldn't want me to be alone forever."

Jenny had to stop for a moment, wipe her eyes, blow her nose. "I will *never* forget David! How *could* I? Your father was wonderful. We had a beautiful life and he gave me you. You two have grown up and you don't need your mama anymore. I couldn't be prouder of you, and I know your dad would be proud, too, that you're making your own way. What I mean is that I want a partner, someone to spend my days with. I want what I thought I'd have with your dad."

Her throat closed up and the tears she'd been holding back began to fall. Jenny couldn't continue; it was more painful than she had expected to say the words aloud. She'd been thinking them for weeks, but making it public – even if only to her boys – felt so real, and the future seemed suddenly so scary. What if it was too late? What if there wasn't someone else for her?

"Aw, Mom, don't cry!" Ryan was always distressed by his mom's tears. He hated seeing anyone cry, but especially his mom. His mom should be happy, she deserved to be happy. He was at her side and engulfing her in a big hug before she could blink. "It's okay. Josh and I want you to be happy – more than anything, right Josh?" Josh was there, too, hugging her and reassuring her that of course, they wanted her to be happy.

"So you – you won't be mad if I…I start looking. I'm not replacing your father…"

"Ma, please, we know…we know…" Josh was tearing up, too.

Karen stood aside and watched these young men give Jenny exactly what she needed – the reassurance that it was alright to move ahead, and their blessing to do just that. She didn't think Jenny knew just how much she'd wanted her boys to support this decision, and Karen was pleased they could give her the support she needed. She was teary herself, truth be told, but she hated crying, so before the scene got too much out of hand, she interrupted.

"Dessert, anyone? I see strawberry shortcake in the fridge…"

Chapter 5

"Are you going to make me stand in the hot sun all day?" she called. Jenny was actually relishing the warmth of the late afternoon, and enjoying to her weekly gardening lessons with Andrew. They'd established a routine, and Friday was gardening day. She'd gotten to the point that she could do much more on her own now, and found herself wandering the yard in the mornings taking note of what needed to be done. Andrew was a good teacher, and she was an eager student. She might not need him next year after all, but she wasn't going to give him up yet. She enjoyed the time they spent together. She felt content when she was with him.

Andrew was making his way up the walk, shielding his eyes from the bright sun, and caught sight of this lovely lady, waiting to garden in… a dress?

"Mrs. M., I hate to tell you this, but if we're going to be in the dirt weeding, your pretty dress is going to be a muddy mess when we finish. It rained last night, remember?"

"Oh I know! But dresses are comfy, and this is an old one. I don't mind if it gets just a bit messy." She was smiling in anticipation.

"Alrighty, then. Let's get started. We're going to the corner, and we'll work our way out. You take the left on your own today, and I'll take the right. It shouldn't take too long. The rain did half our job for us last night." He smiled and set to work picking out the odd weeds and deadheading the flowers.

Jenny stood behind him for just a moment, watching him go to work. She found herself watching him a lot lately. She'd only just admitted it to herself. She watched him through the kitchen window as she made dinner on Tuesdays. She knew it wasn't just casual curiosity for gardening either. Karen called him an Adonis. But Karen was slightly lecherous, too! Jenny only knew that he was… interesting. She was fascinated by the play of lean muscles under his shirt, by the lines of his profile as he worked. Jenny settled in to her side and started the tedious process of deadheading the petunias and geraniums.

They stood at the sink cleaning up after a successful hour of gardening when a thought occurred to her. "Andrew, are you going to be in town next weekend? I'm going to spend the holiday with Ryan, and I need someone to look in on the house. Would you mind?" Karen usually watched her house for her, but this time she wanted to ask him.

"Uh, sure, I guess. I'm here anyway. I never go out of town for the Fourth. Actually, my parents are coming up. So yeah, I can do it. What, exactly, did I just sign up for – you don't have a reptile room, do you?" Andrew was certain she didn't have any furry friends, and remembered her aversion to crawling things. He couldn't help but tease her.

"No snakes! You know I can't stand those things!" She'd squealed like a little girl the one time she'd seen (or thought she'd seen) a garter snake disappearing under the fence. He'd insisted there was no snake, but she wasn't so sure. "It's the easiest job you'll have all summer. Just collect the mail, maybe hang out for an hour or so in the evening. Seriously, just keep it looking lived in. I know it's silly. No one is going to break in, but it will make me feel better knowing you're here. Thank you." She smiled and dried her hands.

"If you don't mind me asking, why me and why not Josh or Karen?"

"Well, for one thing, Karen will be out of town, too. But Josh, well, he lives about 30 minutes away, and it would be inconvenient. He comes over less and less. I don't know if you'd noticed since you aren't usually around when he is anyway. He's busy with his own life, and even though he hasn't said anything, I think he has a girlfriend." Her mouth lifted in a half-smile. "Anyway, I just thought…well you're right here. I think. Actually, I don't really know; where do you live?" She hoped she wasn't being nosy. She found herself more and more curious about this young man. She wanted to know more about him than what he shared on Tuesdays. A lot more.

"I'm in my grandparent's old house. Two blocks away, actually. So yeah, I'm right here." He smiled, encouraged by her curiosity, even if it wasn't romantically motivated.

"You'll need a key." She walked to the key hook. "It'll work on the front door, or the kitchen door. Mail can just be piled up on the table. I don't imagine there'll be much of it, but you never know. And if you can do a quick walk-through every day – again, yes, I know no one is going to break in, but it makes me feel better." She laughed at herself for being such a goose. "I don't want some convict hiding out in my room, waiting to attack me. If I am murdered in my sleep when I get home, I will be sure to haunt you. Got it?"

"Got it, Mrs. M. No murdering criminals allowed." She sure was funny; living alone didn't seem to bother her at all, but being gone for a few days turned her into a worry-wart. Interesting. And endearing. "Don't worry about anything. I'll make sure your place is locked up tight, and you'll be safe from marauders when you get home - and snakes." He added with a wink.

The holiday-weekend celebration was one of the things Jenny missed about the old house. They used to have a cook-out every year. From the back yard, they could see the town fireworks perfectly. It was a great weekend and her favorite part of summer. Last year, they'd tried to re-invent the cook-out and party, but it wasn't the same at all. So this year, she was going to get the heck out of Dodge, and try a different approach altogether. Ryan's big-city digs would be just the thing – a different setting, new people, and no responsibility at all.

Ryan's roommates seemed nice, and the house really was as lovely as he'd said. Big open rooms with an airy feel, it was the most put-together looking bachelor pad she'd ever seen. The furniture actually went together!

Jenny even commented on it when Ryan was giving her the tour. He only laughed and said that Jason's girlfriend had done the shopping for them – with Jason's credit card, of course. When they got married, and they'd probably get married, all the furniture would be going with them. But until then, they had a great place.

"Sweetie, I really want to cook dinner for you all. A thank you for letting me visit. And for letting me commandeer your room while I'm here. What would you like me to cook? Fish? Chicken? What's your favorite nowadays?"

"Mom, you don't have to cook. You're my guest! We can go out for dinner. There is a great Chinese place right around the corner."

"Are you sure? I like cooking! And there's no one to cook for at home." She almost mentioned Andrew, but she stopped short. Ryan might not like that she'd adopted a surrogate son since her own weren't around anymore. And lately, she hadn't felt particularly motherly. It was more an odd kind of friendship. One she cherished, and wasn't ready to share. Not yet.

"No, Mom, no cooking. Let me take care of you this week. Deal?" Ryan wanted his mom to relax. She was always taking care of everyone else. He was going to make sure she enjoyed her time away from home. There were museums to see, a parade to watch, and, of course, burgers and fireworks on the Fourth. She was going to have fun, and forget how much she missed the old days.

"Deal. Although I'm making breakfast at least once. When was the last time you had my pancakes, hmm?" Jenny walked away before he could put up any argument, and went to change for dinner with her son.

"Pancakes, eggs, bacon… I'm in heaven!" Brent was the most over-the-top charmer Jenny had met in a long time. If she didn't know better, she'd swear he was Karen's son. Jenny just chuckled and shook her head.

"More bacon, Brent?"

"Oh, Mrs. Martin, you sure know your way to a man's heart. Yes, please. Ryan, I may have to steal your mama away and marry her."

"Uh, yeah, I don't think so, buddy. Mom, don't pay any attention to him. Your pancakes are every bit as delicious as I remember, though. Thanks for breakfast. Love ya." He gave her a quick squeeze and glared at Brent over her head. He was very proud of his mom, and that his friends enjoyed her cooking and company. They'd had a great time this week spending time together after so long. He hadn't spent this much time with his mom since the summer after his dad had died. He was pleased that she had come, and that he'd been able to show her around town and show her how much he'd grown up since graduation. He liked to think he'd grown and changed. But one thing hadn't changed – his fierce protection of his mother. She was sweet and tender, and completely oblivious to the effect she had on men. Josh and Ryan were used to their friends meeting Mom and being immediately smitten. They were also used to making it abundantly clear that Mom was strictly off limits. He'd had more than a few scuffles with unwise boys who'd had the balls to call his mom a MILF to his face. He was glad she'd be leaving this afternoon. Any more ribbing, and Brent might end up with a black eye. He'd hate for his mom to see that.

Jenny would be home tonight. Andrew stopped at the house to do one last mail pick-up and walk-through. The first day had been strange, and he'd felt awkward being in her house without her. Whenever he'd done work here, she'd been home in case he'd had questions. Tonight, he felt less like an interloper, and as he did his walk-through, he took his time. He looked at the photos displayed around the living room and on the walls of the hallway. He could see her in each nook and corner of her home. Her home reflected her character in every way. It was warm, cozy, and inviting. The furniture and its arrangement put the guest at ease, and there was an indefinable *something* that was *Jenny*.

He was still reluctant to invade her inner sanctum and he debated whether to check the bedroom for critters, reptiles and criminals. In the end, he decided against it. He opened the door. She could assume he'd checked if she wanted, but he kept his eyes averted. *Andrew, you are an idiot. It's just another room.* He knew he was being ridiculous. But he couldn't help it, and he couldn't explain it, even to himself. He just knew that he didn't want to see (was afraid he might see) that she was still hopelessly devoted to her husband. He didn't want to see her room as a shrine to his memory.

Andrew placed his house key on the kitchen table next to the mail where she would be sure to see it. He locked the kitchen door and pulled it closed behind him. Time for a beer with the guys. Whenever he found himself getting too sappy over Jenny, he'd go out for a reality check. She was just not into him, and he was going to find another girl.

When Jenny got home she sorted through the mail and let her mind wander. Andrew had been here, and not too long ago. She could feel it in the air and there was something… something that tickled at the edge of her thoughts, only Jenny couldn't put her finger on it quite yet. She laid down the post and grabbed her bag. It was late, and time for bed. She'd have time to think tomorrow. As she moved through the house, she was comforted by the thought that he'd checked in for her, assuaging her silly fears of intruders. She dumped her bag at the bedroom door and undressed at the edge of the bed. One benefit of living alone was that if she wanted to forego personal hygiene for one night, there was no one to know. She was tired – she'd sleep now, and wash her face and brush her teeth in the morning.

As she drifted off to sleep, the thought that had tickled at the back of her mind came forward. The kitchen, the house… that's what was different. It smelled like…him.

Chapter 6

Son of a bitch, his head hurt. Andrew woke up to the brightest sunrise imaginable, shining right in his face. He buried his head under a pillow and tried falling back to sleep. The pounding in his head, though, was insistent. *This is why we never get drunk,* the smart-ass voice in his head told him. *Oh, shut up,* he told the voice. Andrew hated when the voice was right. Going bar-hopping with the guys, oh, was that ever a bad idea. Maybe next time he'd be the designated driver. If there was a next time. Right now, he felt like the puked up contents of a skunk's belly. At least he remembered everything. *Oh, Lord...* He remembered, alright...grinding with all the girls, and yep, even kissing a few of them. At least he hadn't brought one home this time. *Son of a bitch…*

He gingerly opened his eyes again. The sun had moved sufficiently that it was no longer blinding. *Coffee.* It was the only thing he could think of at the moment. Coffee and a few Tylenol would take the edge off his pounding head. Andrew scooted to the edge of the bed and slowly rolled out.

On the kitchen table was a bright pink piece of paper with a phone number written in the middle. *Just perfect.* He may not have brought a girl home, but he hadn't come away empty-handed. Damn, a number with no name. He couldn't put a name to a single pair of lips he'd kissed, much less the grinder girls…looks like he didn't remember *quite* everything.

His phone buzzed on the charger. No rest for the weary, it seemed. Andrew answered with the best wide-awake voice he could manage.

"Good morning, Andrew! Thank you for house sitting! No burglars, no snakes, no critters. You are wonderful! How can I thank you?"

"No need at all. It was my pleasure."

"Would you like to come over for dinner tonight? It is beautiful outside, let's grill out! I'll have Karen and Danny over, I'll see if I can get Josh to come and bring that elusive girlfriend he's been hiding. I only wish I could've brought Ryan home with me. Please say yes.

You know you want to." Andrew smiled in spite of himself. Her teasing and infectious tone were no match for a hangover.

"Yes, yes, I'll be there. Tell me what time, and what to bring." *And then let me nurse my head in quiet.* No sooner had he hung up with Jenny than the phone buzzed again. Mrs. Newell… "I'll be right there, ma'am." Andrew staggered to the shower to begin his morning. Things didn't look good for a relaxing Saturday afternoon. It was going to be a long, long day.

"Josh, it's been really good seeing you and catching up. Seems like things are really coming together for you." Josh and Andrew were standing along the fence, watching the others play one last round of croquet. The evening had been far better than Andrew had expected. His hangover had dissipated sometime in the early afternoon, and he'd been able to enjoy the impromptu cookout.

"Yeah, it's good." Josh kept his eyes on the slight blonde he'd brought with him. "What do you think – isn't she great? I'm gonna marry that one. I know we haven't dated long, but when you know, you know, right? Only problem is, she's moving. Has a job transfer coming. Houston. I gotta make it official fast."

"Seriously? Houston is a long way away. I take it if you pop the question, you'll be moving, too. I guess you've done some prospecting there, jobs and such?" Andrew was floored. Both that Josh would broach the subject with him, and that Josh was considering such a move. He had always been the one to check up on Jenny, keeping close in case she needed anything.

"Yeah… I've had a couple phone interviews… nothing yet, but I'm looking. You think my mom will be okay? A year ago I wouldn't have considered moving. She was still so fragile. But now look at her. She's…she's like a new person. Ya know?" Josh watched his mom as she laughed over some comment Karen had just made. It was good to see her so happy again. She looked up and caught his eye, and her smile brightened. *Ah, Mom…it's good to have you back.*

"Yeah, I've noticed, too. Everyone has. But don't worry about her. She can take care of herself, and she has Karen and Danny, and…all her friends." *She has me.* "I like Emily. She really suits you. You'd better ask her, before she wises up!" He gave Josh a nudge in the ribs.

"Hey now! I'm a catch, too! I only need to talk to my mom. Hold my beer, I'm gonna take care of it right now. Hey, Ma, come here for a sec, will ya?" Jenny wandered over with a knowing smile on her face and accompanied her son into the kitchen.

"Sweetheart, before you say anything at all, I think she's a keeper. I've seen how you look at her, and how she looks at you. I cannot believe you waited so long to introduce us. But I'll forgive you if you marry her. I'll have plenty of time to get to know her after you're married." Jenny was engulfed in a bear hug before she could blink.

"Aw Mom, I'm so glad you like her! I knew you would. She's awesome. But about getting to know her… Em is moving to Houston. I'm looking for a job there, too, so I can move with her. I hope you'll still be happy for us." Josh pulled away and clasped her hands, looking into his mom's face to gauge her reaction.

"Oh, Baby…moving…? Well, it may take me some time, but I will be happy for you. You must live your own life, and I can take care of me. Now hug your mama, and let's get back out there. It's getting late, and I expect that everyone will be leaving soon." Jenny patted his cheeks as she'd done when he was little, and pulled him in for one more quick embrace.

Karen and Danny left first, followed by Josh and Emily. Andrew was on his way out, too, eyes on Josh's taillights. "Thanks for dinner. I had a great time tonight. I haven't seen Josh for so long, I'd almost forgotten what he looked like. I'll see you on Tuesday?" He glanced back when he heard no response. Jenny was staring blankly at the kitchen sink.

Andrew moved to Jenny's side and wrapped her in his arms. "Hey, you. Come here. Josh is fine – it'll be fine. You'll see." *Ah, but I might not be. I should think before acting.* Jenny felt wonderful in his arms. He dropped them as soon as he could – an appropriately friendly hug, concerned but not overly so.

"Thank you, Sweetie. I know he'll be fine. I was actually thinking of David. He would have loved meeting Emily. She's sweet and cute, and he would have enjoyed bantering with her. I never thought I would be watching my family grow without him." She smiled wistfully, then heaved a sigh and shook off the melancholy. "Yes, well! Thanks for coming. I'll see you on Tuesday."

"Alright, I'll see you. Lock up behind me. You don't want the burglars to getcha." With that teasing remark he closed the door and headed home.

How early is too early to call on a Sunday? Andrew had the phone number in his hands, ready to dial. He couldn't remember her name, but figured he may as well give it a shot. Seeing Josh and Emily together had made him ache yet again for a girl of his own. And if it couldn't be Jenny, maybe this mystery girl was the one. He wouldn't know unless he tried.

Chapter 7

Jenny was bustling in the kitchen, listening to the bird chatter filtering in through the open windows. It was a gorgeous day. Not too hot, but warm, and the sun was shining. She was going to bring some roses in today. There were finally enough on the trellis that she wouldn't strip it bare by cutting a few, and they'd look so lovely in her crystal vase. She had forgotten all about the thing until she'd moved. But it really was a good piece, the perfect size, not too big and not too small. David had given it to her for one of their anniversaries, and she tried to use it as much as possible now that she'd found it.

Her mind was full of thoughts of him today. Some days were just like that. Reaching for the vase on the table, she grasped the neck and swung around to the sink. Realizing, too late, that her grasp was just a little too casual. The vase went crashing onto the tile and splintered into millions of tiny pieces. Jenny stared at the floor and the winking shards, shining like ice on a winter's day.

Without any warning at all, the tears came. Silently at first, then with great waves of sobs, the broken place in her heart was torn open all over again. *David…David I miss you!* One more piece of their life together was broken beyond repair, and she cried for the loss.

Andrew heard the crash just as he entered the garden, and sprinted the rest of the way to the door. It was probably nothing, but just in case…

Jenny was standing in the middle of the kitchen in her bare feet, broken glass surrounding her, her hands still outstretched as though she could catch what was dropped. She looked as though she'd just lost a priceless treasure. The tears were falling unchecked onto her cheeks. *Aw Hell…*

He picked his way over to her, careful to avoid what glass he could, and touched her arm.

"Mrs. M.? Jenny? Are you okay? Are you cut?" He did a quick once over, but he didn't see any blood, thank God. Just to be safe, she needed to leave the kitchen. It looked like it was up to him to move her. He bent down, put his arms around her, and gently picked her up. She didn't say a word, only lay her head against his shoulder, and put her arms around his neck.

Andrew again picked his way carefully across the floor and carried her to the sofa. He sat her in his lap and held her while she continued to cry. She buried her head in his shoulder and turned into him, desperate for comfort. He had never seen anyone so broken. He was shattered and aching for her, and he didn't even know what was wrong. This couldn't possibly be over a broken glass. He comforted her the only way he knew how, stroking her back, her hair, and whispering whatever words of comfort and endearment he could think of. "Aw Sweetheart, I'm sorry… just cry, it's okay to cry sometimes." He said all the things his mom had said to him when he was little and she'd comforted his heartbreaks.

Slowly the tears ebbed, the sobs became hiccups and sniffles. Jenny recognized that she had just poured out all her tears on Andrew's shoulders.

"Oh dear Lord, oh Heavens to Betsy." Jenny wasn't sure what to apologize for first – the fact that his shirt was partially soaked, or the fact that she had just come apart, or the fact that she was still sitting on his lap. Well that last was easily remedied – she scrambled to her feet and smoothed her skirt and wiped the last of her tears from her cheeks. She could barely look at him, she was so mortified.

"Oh my gosh, Andrew, I am so sorry! I never cry like that. I am so…I don't even know what to say…I'm just so sorry."

He stood up with her, standing close and touched a hand to her cheek.

"Jenny…please don't. There is absolutely nothing to be sorry for. Are you alright, though? Need to talk about something? Whatever you need." He dipped his head lower to see her better, but she would have none of it.

She averted her face and backed toward the hallway, wanting to hide. How she'd be able to face him again she didn't know.

"Oh, no. No… I'll be fine. Really. Just… I don't know what came over me. And I must be quite a fright." Jenny always looked like a beet when she cried, and all of a sudden she was very aware of how awful she must look! "Oh, I need to…" Her hands fluttered around her as she trailed off.

"You look fine. But why don't you just go put a cold cloth over your eyes and lie down for a while? You'll feel so much better." And he could cool down a bit. He hoped to God she hadn't noticed that, despite the situation and her tears, he'd been unable to control the reaction of his body to her nearness. He felt like a pervert getting hard when she was clearly so distraught. It wasn't that he was aroused, but… sometimes his parts had a mind of their own, no matter what his brain tried to say.

Jenny fled to her room and closed the door, glad for the excuse he'd provided for not coming out again until he was well and truly gone. *Oh. My. God. What was that all about?* She would love to have the ground open up and swallow her whole. To say she was mortified was an understatement. She understood that grief could come on suddenly, she remembered that from the first year and she'd experienced it more than once, even since then. It had just been a long time. And she had never bawled all over a stranger before. Oh, alright – he was nowhere near a stranger, but still! He was a friend, a very new friend. Only her closest family had seen her like that, and even then she had been distressed at showing her deepest grief. She only hoped they could pretend it hadn't happened. As awkward as it had been to realize that she was sitting in his lap and crying her eyes out, that was less awkward than realizing that at the end, she hadn't wanted to move. He had been very… comfortable… and strong… and he smelled good. Oh God, why did she have to go and notice *that*?

Andrew watched her go, and turned to see what he could do about the mess in the kitchen. Whatever had happened, she'd been beyond upset, and he didn't want her to have to deal with it again. Maybe if he cleaned up all that glass, it would help. He rummaged for the dustpan and broom, and set about putting the kitchen back to rights, before letting himself out. He'd tell her about his date with Abby another time.

Jenny stood in the shower letting the water stream over her. Lost in thought, she hadn't even begun to wash her hair. She'd woken this morning from a dream about Andrew. She didn't think she'd ever dreamt of him before, certainly not that she could remember, and most certainly not like this. Remembering made her skin prickle and her fingers itch.

They'd been talking in the kitchen, about nothing that she could remember, and she'd had the overwhelming urge to lean in and kiss his neck. So she did. In dream-time slow motion. She hadn't touched him in any other way, and he hadn't touched her. If she closed her eyes, she could see it as clearly as if it had happened just a moment ago. She could still see his pulse beating right where she'd placed her lips and could practically feel the heat of his skin, taste the salt of his sweat when she'd touched her tongue to him. The thought of kissing him so intimately made her feel heated all over, and she wanted to do it again.

Chapter 8

Why, oh why was the Reserve not deserted today of all days? On a Sunday morning, everyone should be in church so she could have the park all to herself. Jenny wanted to be quiet and think, and it seemed as if the whole town was out for a Sunday morning stroll. To avoid the crowds, she strode deeper into the Reserve, paths that were less traveled, but also less well marked. She liked the solitude, but hated the feeling that she might just as easily be on a deer path as a walking trail.

Finally, Jenny came upon a clearing, a scenic overlook where she could sit and breathe in the clean air, hear the river rushing below her, and try to sort through the jumble of thoughts running through her head. She chose a small outcropping of rock, dusted it off, and gingerly sat down. It's not so much the dirt that made her wary, but the thought of spiders or other creepy crawlies.

She smiled to herself, thinking of how Andrew would tease her for her aversion to insects. Then she smiled just to think of Andrew. He was the reason she was here, but her smile faded as she thought back on the last twenty-four hours, and then over the last few weeks and months.

Yesterday had been a revelation. She'd known that her feelings for him were beyond simple maternal caring, making sure to carefully categorize them as friendship. But it was clear that her feelings were more than either of those. She was… fond of him. Enjoyed spending time with him, whether they were gardening or sharing dinner. More and more often, the gardening session or dinner stretched into the evening. They would stay at the table and talk, or sit on the patio and watch the day melt into night. Sometimes they'd watch television, but hardly ever. Perhaps a movie would have felt too much like a date, and they avoided it. They were just two people keeping each other company and staving off loneliness. It was something they'd talked about – being lonely, even among a crowd. Jenny was glad to find someone who seemed to understand her, without trying to change her or cheer her up. Lately, too, she hadn't needed to be cheered up. Her spirits were buoyed just thinking of him, and looking forward to Tuesdays and Fridays. It should have been an indicator. How had she missed it? *You didn't miss it. You just didn't want to think about it. Face it, you don't want to scare him off, and you're afraid of what will happen if he knows you have feelings for him.* Having secret and tender feelings for someone was something she hadn't had to deal with since she was a girl. It was scary! She felt like she was in middle school all over again. What if he didn't like her back? What if he only wanted to continue as friends – or worse – what if he didn't want to be friends anymore? She felt 14 instead of 45, young and unsure and completely out of her depth. Jenny sat there for a long time, dwelling on the what-ifs, thinking back on special moments with Andrew.

She thought of the day they tried grilling for the first time. The burgers were wonderful, and he took full credit, crowing like a rooster at the accomplishment of cooking with fire. Never mind that she'd used her secret recipe to hand make each one, and had made all the side dishes as well. But they had laughed and carried on arguing who was the better cook all evening. She remembered the way he preened when she'd admired his brute strength while rearranging her patio planters. She thought of him remembering his grandparents, relating anecdotes of them, and tearing up one day when he'd especially missed his Gramps.

Finally she thought about yesterday. He'd been so gentle with her, soothing her, coaxing her through the torrent of her tears. He was a beacon of light at the end of a long tunnel – not just yesterday, but all through her spring awakening. This was no simple crush, not at all. He'd become…well, if not her reason for living, the main reason she'd begun to live again.

Lost in thought, Jenny failed to notice that she was no longer alone on the lookout. Andrew stood to the side, wondering whether to alert her to his presence or not. He came here when he wanted to ponder things, and as far as he knew, it was a forgotten section of trail. He'd never seen another person here in all the time he'd been coming, and was stunned to see the very woman he'd come to ponder. Before he could talk himself out of it, he moved toward her. Even though she had presumably come for solitude, she was in his spot! It had to be an omen. Andrew called softly to her and slid next to her on the rock.

"Hey. How are ya, Sweetheart?" He lifted her hand and laced his fingers with hers. He had never been so familiar with her, but today it felt right. As though every boundary they'd set between them had been set aside yesterday. They were only Andrew and Jenny. She was the woman he loved. He only hoped he could be the man she'd love. They sat in silence. He didn't dare speak, for fear that he would frighten her off.

Jenny stared in wonder at their hands. As if he'd been summoned by her thoughts, Andrew was here beside her, clasping her hand and sharing the silence. She placed her free hand atop their two and returned her gaze to the river. It was too much for her to speak, and she wasn't sure just what to say, anyhow. Tears welled up against her will. Hadn't she cried enough yesterday? At least they didn't spill over this time. As they sat, her focus returned again and again to their hands. They fit together perfectly, and it felt natural. Jenny thought it was an outward sign of how their personalities entwined, too. They…fit together. *Like two pieces of a puzzle. Tell him…*

"Andrew…I…" *I don't know what to say. Dear Lord, Help.*

"It's okay. You don't have to say anything. I came here to be alone and think, too. I didn't imagine I'd see you, or anyone, actually. Would you rather I go? I can go…" He loosened his grip on her hand. Better to leave than have her tell him to go.

"No. No, please stay. It is nice to…to have a friend…" *Not a friend. Jenny, tell him.* "I, um, I was thinking about you. About yesterday." She tightened her hands, pulling him close again, and looked into his eyes, then looked quickly away, afraid that everything would be shining for him to see. Afraid he would pull away if he saw.

"Jenny, please don't apologize again. That's what friends do, right? Friends are there for each other." The fact that she wanted him to stay as a friend, well, it was something to work with. He needed to tell her. But he had no words.

"No, I won't apologize – and yes, that's what friends do. I am glad for your friendship. Andrew, you are... Thank you." *Thank you? That's what you have to say? Jenny!* She groaned inwardly at her lack of courage. Then latched onto something that had finally struck her. "Andrew, you called me Jenny. Not Mrs. Martin, not Ms. M." A slow smile appeared on her face. She whispered, "Jenny. It's about time."

"You bawled all over me. I think it does away with any formality I was trying to hold onto. You don't mind? Really?" *Thank God.*

"I don't mind. I like it. And calling me Sweetheart." Surely that would be a hint.

"Oh, that! That was probably a little too...I'm sorry."

"No, I...I liked it. It's just..." She spoke shyly, trying so hard to convey her hopes without saying anything damning.

Before he thought to stop himself, Andrew leaned over and pecked her cheek. "I suppose it's been a while since anyone's called you Sweetheart. Well, I guess I can start..." He tried for a teasing tone, unsure how much he could get away with. He wanted to scoop her back onto his lap for a proper kiss. He wanted to tell her how much he needed her. But he only sat there, holding her hand, and hoping she would someday understand and love him in return.

Well, that was a chaste and filial kiss... Face it, Jen. He may be your friend, but that's all. Look, he's so calm. No sparks for him. Put it out of your mind. Jenny strove for a friendly smile and nudged his shoulder. Then returned her gaze once again to the river, as heavy-hearted and confused as she'd been when she'd arrived. At least she had a friend to hold her hand while she figured things out.

At first, Jenny felt as though she'd lost a valuable opportunity to talk to Andrew at the river. But she didn't know what she would have said, or how he would have reacted. Perhaps he would have been horrified – a woman her age, with him? The more she thought about it, the more glad she was that she'd not said a word. He might set her heart fluttering, but it still felt odd, whenever she put her mind to it, to think about their respective ages. And she became more and more set in her mind that he could never – *would* never – find her attractive. How could he? She was old, compared to him. She was a *mom* – not just any mom, but a friend's mom. He made her feel young, but facts were facts, and she was almost twenty years older than he. It was so easy to forget because she didn't *feel* old when she was with him. She felt like herself, happy in his company. Ever since Karen had put the thought in her head, she'd been 'ogling' him. Not that she did it when he'd notice! He was a superior male specimen, and so sweet. Then he'd held her, and she could hardly think of him without wondering what it would be like if he kissed her.

Maybe it was time to ask Karen about those dates. Perhaps she could find a man her *own* age that would set her heart aflutter, too. She needed to give it a shot, because she couldn't spend the second half of her life mooning after a dream.

"Jenny, I found the perfect man – and you're meeting him after work tomorrow for drinks." Jenny and Karen were out for a walk at the Reserve. "He's tall, dark, and handsome, impeccable manners, a true gentleman. You're going to love him!" Karen was all abuzz over this man. She was sure he'd be great for Jen and a good companion with whom to begin the dating process. And if they fell in love and got married, well…they'd cross that bridge when they got there. But then, there was also Andrew. She'd kept an eagle-eye on them at Jenny's cookout. It was odd that they got on so well, and seemed quite happy with each other, yet neither seemed to realize that the other was interested. How could two people be quite so clueless?

"Oh, Karen, I couldn't possibly tomorrow. Tuesdays are my day with Andrew, remember? I couldn't cancel dinner with him on short notice like that. How about Wednesday? You and Danny can join us. Come on! You know you want to." She teased Karen, knowing her friend would be beside herself with knowing every detail of the date.

"No, nope – not touching that with a ten-foot pole. Danny and I are not double-dating with you. He will kill me for setting you up in the first place! He hates when I play matchmaker. But I love you, Sweetie. You will call me immediately after he leaves, you have to promise!" She didn't miss Jenny's objection to giving up an evening with Andrew. *Andrew again? Hmm…*

Tuesday night came, and Jenny waited in the kitchen, impatient for Andrew to arrive. He always came, but today she worried he wouldn't. She had news. Finally, finally, a date! She wanted him to be excited for her. Jenny had so many hopes, though she tried *not* to hope. It was her first date, after all, but a girl couldn't help it. Would Gary make her heart skitter? She hoped she'd be just as excited to see him as she was to see Andrew. Andrew was simply much too young. Maybe Gary could be the cure for her crush.

There he was. She could see him through the kitchen window, brushing the dust of the day from his denim-clad thighs. Jenny turned from the window, hoping he hadn't seen her looking. She unconsciously patted her hair, smoothing the flyaways and tightening the ponytail with a quick tug.

"Jenny, tell me. I can see you're dying to tell me something exciting." Andrew suppressed a chuckle and his eyes danced in anticipation. She looked ready to burst with some news. Perhaps Josh had gotten a job offer in Houston.

Jenny practically bounced in her seat. "Guess what. No, I'll tell you. I have a date tomorrow. His name is Gary. Karen set us up and she was so gush-y. He sounds like a dream." Her bright eyes and warm smile dimmed slightly as she tried to decipher his expression. His smile had faltered and it was missing in his eyes now.

"Oh, Jenny, that's great." He felt compelled to say something encouraging, but he felt anything but. When she'd talked about dating, it had been hypothetical and abstract. Now that it was real, he wanted to tell her no. *No, it isn't great, because I want you for myself. I don't want our time together to end.*

After dinner they sat under the pergola and listened to the silence of the settling evening. There was a tension tonight and Jenny didn't know how to address it. Andrew had been reluctant in his excitement for her. His words said he was glad for her, but his eyes had said something else. Could he not see that she was eager to begin again? Or worse, did he think she shouldn't? She'd give her right arm to know what he was really thinking.

"Andrew," Jenny began, "you seem, I don't know, a little tense tonight. Something going on at work? Or maybe," a thought occurred to her. "You don't know Gary do you? If you did, and he's not a great guy, you'd tell me, right?"

"Oh, Sweetheart." Andrew deliberately used the endearment, hoping to pull at her heart. "If Karen was excited for you, he's probably a stand-up guy. She knows you. She'd never set you up with a jerk." Though he jealously hoped Gary was a complete loser and Jenny would come to him for sympathy afterward. He was such a hypocrite, wanting Jenny's date to be a miserable failure, all the while hoping that seeing Abby would cure him of this crazy infatuation. *Seeing Abby – as if one date is actually seeing her. Did you call her back? No, because she's not Jenny. Who's the jerk?*

Chapter 9

"I don't know, Karen. He was nice, just like you said – a perfect gentleman, handsome. A great catch, I know." Jenny and Karen were taking their usual route through the reserve. Jenny had told her all about the evening with Gary, every detail, from what she wore, to what they'd eaten, every word spoken that she could remember. It had been, on paper, a successful first date. He'd come to her door with flowers in hand, earnest and nervous, and quite adorable in that sense. It had actually set her at ease, and she'd gone out of her way to put him at ease, too. He'd taken her to a lovely little restaurant where they could talk and enjoy their meal. He was a pleasant conversationalist, and they had a few common interests, but…

"I don't get it." Karen said. "I thought you'd do well together. And you're telling me you had a good time, so what's the problem?"

As if on cue, Andrew came into sight from the other direction on the path. Karen noticed that Jenny's eyes locked onto him and were immediately averted. She'd turned a lovely shade of pink. He didn't stop this time, but smiled and ran on. Karen made a show of turning to watch his backside as he kept on. "That is one fine ass. And the rest of him…yum. I think I'll have to request he work shirtless in my house from now on." She glanced at Jenny, who still hadn't looked up, and whose color had flared from lovely pink to bright red. "Come on, Jenny, I'm only joking. I think Danny might have an objection to it, anyway." Not even a smile. *Good grief.*

Jenny was feeling just a little weak-kneed. Sometimes she was shocked at how much she desired Andrew, and seeing him today had taken her by surprise. She wanted to do all sorts of wicked things to him and with him. Occasionally, like today, her hormones were wild, and it took everything she had to corral them and keep them under wraps. Seeing him half-naked and glistening with sweat – *Oh, my gosh. Settle down, Jenny. You're not an alley cat.*

"Well, then, back to Gary. Are you going to go out with him again? Or should I break the bad news gently?"

"Break it gently," she said, trying desperately to sound casual. "He's nice, but he's not…" *Not Andrew.*

"Right. Not the one. Okay. I'll try again. Promise. We'll find Mr. Wonderful, don't worry." *Or at the very least, you'll see that your Mr. Wonderful is right under your nose.* Karen thought again about Jenny's odd behavior moments ago. She was normally so bright when they saw Andrew, and today, she could barely look at him. And he was so hot! It was definitely odd. Was she trying *not* to notice him?

Karen concocted a plan. It wasn't a very good plan, according to Danny, who was against plans like this anyway. Why she'd told him, she didn't know. He objected heartily to blind dates and thought Jenny could manage just fine on her own. But if Jenny couldn't see what was staring her right in the face with Andrew, *someone* had to help her see it.

"So…Karen tells me you're an architect. That sounds interesting." Jenny only needed this one conversation starter to get the man to talk the rest of the evening. Karen had some explaining to do. The man was an absolute bore. Not that he didn't tell great stories, but he had no interest in anyone but himself! *Ugh…*

"So, Karen tells me you're a lawyer – that sounds interesting."

The lawyer launched into an hour-long monologue about his job. Jenny had been on this very date last week with an architect, and the week before that with a psychologist. Did Karen only know men who were puffed up, arrogant weenies who thought they were God's gift to woman-kind? *Good grief.*

Jenny spent the remainder of the evening admiring the dresses of women walking by and wondering what Andrew was doing. She missed him. She missed how they used to talk. Things had been just a little bit strained ever since she'd started dating, and more often than not, dinner was cancelled by one or the other of them. Work, they'd say. But she knew it wasn't just work, not for her, anyway. It was the strain of dating other men, and comparing them constantly with him. They always came up just a little bit short. Jenny thought of his reaction if he ever found out she had a schoolgirl crush on him. She was sure he'd be kind, but she couldn't stand the thought that he might pity her for wanting something she couldn't have. He was so young and not for her. *Remember that. He's not for you.*

Afraid she might cry at the depressing thoughts running through her mind, she hastened to put an end to the miserable evening. She was done putting up with the lawyer.

"I'm sorry to interrupt, but I need to go. I have plans for an early morning tomorrow, and I need my beauty rest." Jenny made her excuses and reassured him that there was no need at all to take her home. She left the restaurant as quickly as she could, and walked herself home. This dating business was for the birds.

Chapter 10

Another dream? She only half awoke, then drifted back into it, letting sleep and want carry her away.

He was reaching for her again. He always seemed to appear from nowhere, this misty shadowed lover of hers. His hands were everywhere at once. She could feel her nipples peaking for him as he pulled gently on them with his teeth, one and then the other, fingers mimicking mouth so that neither breast was neglected. She arched into him with a moan, arms cast to each side, fingers twisting in the sheets. The pleasure-pain was exquisite.

His fingers played in her short curls, gliding deftly over her, teasing and spreading the lips, circling her entrance, but never delving into her. Tormenting her so that she begged him, "Please, please. I need more." She wanted to feel him inside her – his fingers, his tongue, his sex. Anything – everything. She wanted all he had to give, and wanted to give all in return. The whisper-soft caresses made her ache all the more, never assuaging the need, only building it.

Jenny's alarm broke into her dream. Her lover disappeared when the loud rock anthem blared from her bedside. Her body was once again on fire, with no one to quench it. *Damn, damn, damn!*

It had been the longest day of a long week. Of course, she didn't *have* to work late, but she enjoyed her job, and lately it helped to keep her mind off her growing discontent. She'd been dating, but no one was right for her. She knew she wasn't being too picky, no matter what Karen said. She would know when he was right. It had only been a few dates, though, so she shouldn't be so frustrated. Jenny just didn't know why she was so frustrated. No, she knew exactly why. She wanted sex, a thought she barely acknowledged to herself. She certainly wasn't going to admit it to Karen. She felt like a horny teenager all the time, and it was extremely uncomfortable. Not to mention embarrassing. She was 45, for Pete's sake; she should have this under control. Except that she hadn't had sex in ages, and her body was clamoring for it again. Worst of all, clamoring for a certain young Adonis. *Oh Jenny – get a grip, and forget him. Young men do not want to date mothers.*

Karen was tired of getting her head bitten off by Jenny. Her friend was never this cranky, and something was obviously eating at her. The trouble was, she wasn't talking. Karen wasn't used to that, either. Jenny was a private person, but she usually told Karen everything. They'd been best friends since grade school, and they each knew the other inside-out. No secrets between them, until lately.

"So…are you going to tell me what's been making you so miserable, or do I have to guess?"

"I'm fine," she snapped. "Just tired. And what's with those guys you keep fixing me up with? They are self-absorbed bores. I know you know me better than that." Jenny latched onto the first plausible reason she could come up with for her grumpiness. She wasn't about to tell Karen that she was horny as hell, and what's more, was mad at herself for wanting Andrew.

"They're all at the top of their fields. What's not to like? Handsome, successful and rich." And completely unimpressive to Jenny, Karen knew. Eventually Jenny would realize that what she really wanted was a young Jack-of-all-trades who was just as smitten as she was, if only she'd look. Karen inwardly sighed. *When Shakespeare said love is blind, I don't think this is what he meant.*

Chapter 11

Jenny was on her way out when she spied movement in the toolshed.

"Halloo? Andrew, is that you?" she called out.

"Hello – hey. Yeah, sorry to bother you so early. I have plans tonight, so I thought I'd come by this morning. Hope you don't mind." *Thank God!* She was finally home. He hadn't seen her in almost an entire month, and was going nuts at the thought.

"Of course it's fine. What's up tonight? Hot date?" she teased. It would do him good to get out – and her, too, if she was perfectly honest. She found herself thinking about him so much more than she should.

Picturing him out on a date with some sweet young thing was, if not entirely comfortable, probably a very good thing. She suppressed the twinge of jealousy she felt at the thought of him with another woman.

"Yeah, actually. I met someone while I was out with the guys. It's a first date, though, so we'll see." He watched her carefully, hoping for some sign that she might care who he was with. Did he imagine that she'd frozen for a moment? She looked sunny, and genuinely pleased for him.

"Good. You boys, mine included, need to start thinking about settling down. Your mama is going to want grandbabies, I know!" She hoped she sounded as motherly as she intended. Her breath had caught at his words, but it's what she'd wanted, wasn't it?

"Uh…I think you might be jumping the gun just a bit – first date, remember?" He smiled good-naturedly at her ribbing. *Good Lord…babies?* He did not want babies, not now, and possibly not ever. He definitely didn't want to think about them on his first date with…Chelsea? Yeah, Chelsea. Well, if ever he needed evidence that Jenny was only mothering him, this was it.

"Right, first date – sorry!" Jenny chuckled and then grew pensive. It was now or never – she needed to make up for the last few weeks. "Andrew, I know we've both been busy lately, but are you available Tuesday for dinner? I have missed our conversations. My last few dates have not understood the art of discourse. Perhaps you can remind me what it's like to be talked *with*, not talked *at*." She hoped she sounded casual, anything to disguise the longing that would surely show in her eyes, if he cared to look. *Please, God – let him think I just want to resume our simple friendship. Please, God – make him say yes!*

Andrew was confused again. Why were women so confusing? But he wasn't going to look a gift horse in the mouth. Whatever else Jenny was, she was a great cook, and he'd be an idiot to turn down dinner.

"Uh, yeah, sure. Of course I can come. Want me to bring anything? I'm good for, well, I can bring beer!" He laughed, and realized that he felt lighter than he had in weeks. It was good to talk to her again. Very good.

The two friends settled back into their routine, almost without a hiccup – dinner on Tuesdays and gardening on Fridays. The first Tuesday had been awkward until Andrew finally asked point blank what all that fuss had been about the day she'd cried all over him.

"Jenny, why were you so upset over a glass? I just don't get it."

She'd wondered if he'd ask about that. She both dreaded and longed to explain. "Ah…that wasn't just glass. It was a crystal vase that David gave me for our fifteenth anniversary. I can't explain why I was so upset over it, exactly. Well, yes, I think I can. It wasn't so much the vase itself, as losing one more reminder of David. I'll never forget him, of course, but our life together is falling farther and farther into my past. I think that's what I was so emotional about. Can you understand that? I'm not sure if I even do." Jenny realized, though, that while she hadn't been able to explain it then, she'd just stumbled into the perfect explanation for herself. It was just this: time was marching on without David, and sometimes it was hard, or painful, or even infuriating that she must march on without him.

He thought of his grandparents, especially Gramps, with whom he'd been so close. "Yeah, I think I do understand a little. Crazy, huh, to think that they've been gone for so long, and yet, sometimes, it seems like only yesterday. Of course, my grandparents lived good long lives, as people like to remind me, and your David didn't. Jenny, I know it was a good life. Just not long enough…" Andrew thought he'd better stop before he made her cry again. Walking to the fridge, he changed the subject. "How about a beer? It's been that kind of day."

"Alright. Tell me about your date. How did it go?" Jenny wasn't sure she really wanted the answer, but true friends were genuinely happy for each other, and if he'd found a girl he liked, then she'd be happy for him. Or at least she would try.

"Oh, you know, it was good. Fine..." He slowly closed the refrigerator door and composed himself. *Really? Jenny, I don't want to talk to you about this.* "She's nice." He pried the tops off the bottles and handed her one before sitting across the table again.

"Nice, huh?"

"Very nice." Andrew smiled, amused in spite of himself at her obvious fishing. "She seemed, yes, very nice. Polite, ladylike, very proper. A girl I would be proud to take home to the parents." She had been all those things, and nothing like the vague recollection he'd had of a wild party girl at the bar. But, then, he hadn't been himself that night, either, so who was he to judge? Perhaps she'd been trying to forget, just as he'd been. It wasn't a topic either of them had brought up, which suited him just fine.

"And pretty? I assume she was pretty..." She trailed off, waiting for him to describe this lovely lady. Jenny fiddled with the label on the bottle as she let the silence grow. She glanced from the bottle to Andrew, caught his eye and quirked an eyebrow, encouraging him to go on.

"Yes, she is pretty. She has dark hair, and blue eyes. She's a little shorter than me, and, well, she's pretty." *And she looks remarkably like you...*

"Andrew, you are not very good at dishing about your date. Was it so bad?" Jenny could only too well imagine, after having been on more than a few dismal evenings herself the last month.

"No, it wasn't bad. It was just… I dunno, we just didn't really click, you know?" *She wasn't you.*

"Yeah, I know. I've been on a few of those. Do you think you'll ask her out again? Maybe give it another shot since she was nice. Sometimes the sparks are slow to kindle." Never mind that she wasn't about to give any of her prospective beaus a second chance.

"Yeah, maybe…maybe I just need to get to know her better. And at least she's nice." *She's not you, but maybe she can help me forget that I want you…*

Jenny continued her first-dates-only marathon. She hadn't had a second date yet, and enjoyed regaling Andrew with her horror stories on Tuesdays. They laughed and joked, and Andrew gave her pointers on dating, mostly outrageous ideas that just made them both giggle. It wasn't Jenny who needed pointers, she asserted, but all her miserable would-be beaus!

Occasionally, one would catch the other looking wistful and would tease the mood away with a joke or change of topic. If there was a charged moment or two, they did their best to ignore it. Andrew was dating Chelsea, and tried his best to channel all his romantic interest toward her. Jenny did her best to be genuinely happy that he'd found a girl who seemed to be perfect for him, and hoped for some semblance of that happiness for herself. If any of her first dates made her feel half as giddy as Andrew did, she would have given them a second date in a heartbeat. The trouble was, no one seemed to measure up to the standard she had set. Just as there had only been one David, there was only one Andrew.

Chapter 12

"That blackberry bramble is just plain useless. You're going to have to get rid of it. It doesn't produce, and it's not going to. If you want, I'll start tearing it out today." Andrew was scowling at the bramble in the corner of the garden. He wasn't sure why it was even there. He didn't remember ever seeing any good berries on it. If there were any, the birds got to them before anyone else could. It would take a couple days, too.

"You're sure? It's a messy job, I can see that from here. But you're right. Go ahead and get rid of it. I'll help however I can."

Jenny watched as Andrew set about cutting out the thorny branches a little at a time and placing them carefully on the wheel barrow, occasionally carting them off to the pick-up in the driveway. She could see that despite the long sleeves and gloves he wore, he would have thorny scratches all over his arms when he was done. Even though she'd offered to help, he insisted on working alone, never asking for a hand. She alternated between watching him and weeding her own little patch of garden until she couldn't stand it anymore.

"Andrew, that's enough for today. Your arms are all cut up, and I can see the bloody scratches from here. Come inside and we'll get you cleaned up. You'll be good to go tomorrow." Of course, tomorrow he'd have new scratches, but she'd just fuss over him again then. She grabbed him by the hand and dragged him inside and to the kitchen sink.

"Here, take off those gloves and wash up. I'll go grab some peroxide to douse those scratches." When she returned he was just drying off.

"Jenny, please. I don't need any of that. Soap and water is good enough."

"Now you listen here, I will not have you getting an infection from those stupid brambles. Let me fuss over you and be done with it. Sit." She smiled to soften the severity in her voice. "You know, wearing long sleeves is pointless if you're going to push them up to your elbows anyway. Silly man. Let me see." Jenny held his hands and turned them over to inspect his forearms. His hands were fine; only his arms were affected, and easily treated. She glanced up at his face. "Oh, Andrew, you've cut your cheek. Doesn't that hurt?" She touched her fingers to the slash of red on his cheekbone.

"It's fine – hardly noticed it. Really." And he hadn't, until she touched it. The peroxide Jenny insisted on dabbing on it stung, but it was nothing to the torment of her nearness. Although they spent time together, they were almost never this close. Before the incident with the broken vase, he'd thought nothing of it, but after he'd held her in his arms, everything had changed. To preserve their truce and friendship, he purposely avoided contact, and he suspected she did the same. He didn't understand her reasons, but his were purely out of self-preservation.

To touch her, to hold her…he was finally accepting that she didn't want more than friendship, and he didn't want to fall down that rabbit hole again. But oh, he caught a glimpse of shadow between her breasts as she leaned over him; the elusive fragrance she wore teased him. Andrew closed his eyes and breathed deeply. It only made him more aware of her. *We are friends, only friends.* He repeated this mantra over and over. It didn't help. He still wanted her. He thanked her for her ministrations and high-tailed it out of the house before he did something he knew he'd regret.

Jenny got ready for bed that night in a trance. She'd remembered too late why she kept her distance from Andrew. Now, her thoughts circled around him, the way his blue eyes lit up with his smile and laugh, the timbre of his voice as he told her about his day. As always, her thoughts circled back to holding his hands. She'd loved the feel of his work-roughened palms under her fingers, the strength that she could both feel and see as she made her inspection. She had longed to place them on her waist and draw him close in her arms. It was while she'd made her inspection that she'd realized she had dreamed of him more than once – many times. She'd recognized the spicy cologne that haunted her in dreams. *His* scent. His were the arms she felt around her, his kisses teased her from sleep, and his lovemaking made her burn at the memory of it. He was her dream lover. Of course he was. *Oh, Dear God…*

"I, um…I broke it off with Chelsea yesterday. It just wasn't working. She's nice and all – just… I dunno. No fireworks." *Not like with you. How can I think of anyone else when I'm with you?*

"Oh, Sweetie, I'm sorry. But I know what you mean. Karen's list has been full of duds so far. No fireworks." *Not like when I'm with you…*

"Well, it's not the end of the world. Tell you what, let's give it another year, and if we haven't found our soulmates by then, we'll marry each other. We get along just fine, don't we?" Andrew wasn't joking. He'd marry her right now, in a heartbeat. But he didn't think she'd be interested, so he used the lightest, most playful tone he could summon. He turned, expecting her to laugh at him and tease him back. Instead, he heard a swift intake of breath, then silence. He could feel the change in her, in the air. Suddenly the room was over-warm and small. His laughter died, and he was all too aware of their solitude and the coming night.

She could feel the tension stretch between them as she turned from the cupboard where she'd just placed the glasses. He moved toward her, slowly, steadily, and with determination in his eyes. She felt like the proverbial deer in the headlights, fixed in place and unable to move. Andrew stopped only inches away, slid his hands down her arms and laced his fingers with hers.

Leaning in so closely that his breath caressed her ear, he murmured, "May I kiss you?" Without waiting for an answer, he trailed his lips deliberately along her jawline, the whisper of touch heightening her sense of anticipation. She raised her chin, inviting him to kiss the sensitive flesh of her neck. He kissed her there, tracing a path downward to her collarbone and returning slowly to the hollow behind her earlobe. Her skin was flushed, her only thoughts focused wherever his lips landed. She could feel the caress of his tongue gently tracing her skin, and wanted – God, she wanted! – to feel his lips on hers.

"Please…" She lifted her hands to his head, slid her fingers through his hair. Holding him to her as his mouth continued its journey, she could feel the slide of his lips, his tongue, the graze of teeth. Her skin was more than flushed. It was on fire. His arms had snaked around her and he held her close. She could feel his hard body against hers from thigh to breast. Again, she whispered, "Please." She turned into him and brought his face to hers, capturing his lips with her own. Jenny couldn't remember the last time she had felt so alive. Andrew's mouth was on hers, and she opened to welcome him in. He traced her lips with the tip of his tongue, and she met him with her own, teasing and tempting him to fence with her. Andrew growled low and she answered with a moan, further invitation to deepen the kiss, to explore what was beyond kisses.

Jenny's hands roved eagerly over his back, up and down, from nape to the small of his back. She was itching to move lower, but that was bolder than she was willing to be. He plundered her mouth, his hands pulling her closer into him, the ridge of his erection pressing against her belly, and his fingers tugging her ever closer. The answering heat pooled at the apex of her thighs and she lifted one leg, wrapping it tightly around him, unconsciously rocking into him.

"My God, Jenny. You're killing me." Andrew pulled his lips away, breath ragged with need, and rested his forehead against hers. "I want you. I love you – let me love you." He reinforced his request with kisses over her neck, moving ever lower. As his fingers pushed aside her blouse, reaching for her breasts with hands and lips, she registered what he'd just said. *He couldn't possibly* – desire was quickly displaced by panic.

"Oh no, no, oh Andrew, no!" She pushed away, and scrambled back. Reality came crashing in as she realized what had just happened. Heavens to Betsy, she'd just been getting it on with someone young enough to be her son! "This is not good! Andrew… I'm not supposed to – I can't get involved with you." She glanced at him beneath her lashes. He looked like he'd been sucker-punched. Jenny turned away, unable to face him.

"Not supposed to… Can't…? Jenny, I thought you wanted this, too. No, I know you do!" He reached for her, winding his arms around her waist and touching his lips to the nape of her neck. "Jenny. We've been dancing around this for weeks."

"No Andrew – I can't do this, not now, and not ever. For Pete's sake, you're almost twenty years younger than me! What will people say?" He felt her shrink from him, pulling away physically and emotionally.

"You're kidding, right? Who the hell cares what people say? They should mind their own damn business! Jenny, you can't kiss me like that and expect that I won't want…Dammit." He abruptly let her go, and she regretted instantly the loss of his warmth, but she didn't turn toward him. "Forget it." Andrew turned on his heel and left without another word. He didn't even slam the door, signaling just how angry he was, and how tightly he held onto his control.

Jenny lost track of how long she stood at the kitchen sink, staring blankly out the window. It wasn't the rising moon and deepening night she saw, but the image of Andrew as he had been just that afternoon, pruning the roses on the trellis, whistling some mindless tune, and looking more handsome than anything she'd ever seen.

She remembered his over-the-shoulder glance, the quick smile hello, and the way his shirt pulled tight over his back as he reached for the farther blooms, emphasizing the vee from his broad shoulders to his slim hips. Jenny was pretty sure he did that on purpose every once in a while, showing off his athletic body, making her want what she shouldn't have.

She enjoyed watching him, though, and talking to him, laughing with him. Until something jolted her back to the present and she realized how old she was next to him. It's not that she didn't want him. He was smart and funny and thoughtful, and handsome as the devil. But, how could he possibly want her? Surely once he saw her, well, she certainly wasn't the young nubile goddess he deserved. Two children and forty-some years tended to add wear and tear to a body. Stretch-marks and scars, cellulite, wrinkles and sagging. Sure, she knew she was pretty enough, and quite presentable in a dress. But to be naked in front of someone – an Adonis like him – no, she would be so self-conscious! Jenny belonged with someone her own age, someone who had his own share of middle-aged-body-ness. Someone who wouldn't care about hers. Unfortunately, she didn't yet know any men her age who made her heart skip a beat. Or who made her skin burn with desire at the mere thought of him, someone who could melt her with a glance and set her on fire with a touch.

Jenny had begun to suspect that Karen was onto her regarding Andrew, and that she pushed all those bores on her, knowing that none of them measured up to him. Karen... matchmaking against the odds. Jenny was certain that as much as she liked Andrew, that path led to sure heartbreak. Time for a phone call. Karen needed to start taking this dating thing seriously, and set her up with some ideal gentleman. But perhaps tomorrow. Tonight, she was going to crawl into bed and cry herself to sleep, mourning yet again for what she couldn't have.

Karen called early. "Where are you? Breakfast, remember? It's Saturday!"

Jenny groaned. After a fitful night of crying and overthinking, Jenny was pretty sure she looked as bad as she felt.

"Ugh, I don't feel so good. I have a headache, and frankly you just woke me up. I'm not going to make it today, okay?"

"Alrighty, then, I'll be right over. I'll bring you coffee and a scone. When you are feeling better, you can eat."

This was just as good a time as any to get a real honest-to-goodness date from Karen. Jenny had to forget *him*. There was no sense in saying no to Karen, anyway. She wouldn't listen, and Jenny didn't have the energy for a fight. Better to just let Karen come over and fuss. It's not like Jenny had lied – she really did have a headache after last night.

Jenny could hear Karen moving in the kitchen. After the phone call, she'd thought she may as well get up and into the shower. Steaming hot water might be just the thing for her head. Unfortunately, though her head felt better, her mind still reeled over what had taken place last night. The reality of Andrew's kiss put her fantasies in the dust.

She ambled in, still in her robe and towel-drying her hair. Karen was puttering around the sink, putting away the last of the dishes and wiping down the counter. She turned her eagle-eye onto Jenny and grinned, "Out with it. Dinner for two last night? I know neither of the boys stopped by or they'd still be here. Who's the secret man – and did he stay the night? Is that why you 'forgot' about breakfast this morning? Had to kick the man out of bed? Oh Jenny – I am surprised! And delighted!"

Her eyes gleamed with mischief at the thought of her sweet friend finally getting back in the game. She hoped her scheming was finally paying off, and that Andrew and Jenny had finally realized the feelings they had for each other. "I want details – well, not too many, but what did he look like? Was it hot? Do I know him? Why are you hiding him? He's not the old grocer that keeps making passes at you is he? Oh Jenny dear, I hope not! That man is old enough to be your dad! Although, granted, he does have all his hair, and a mighty fine smile. I bet he knows his way around the bedroom.

Hmm, if I were single I'd make a pass at him, myself! Ha!"

Karen laughed at her own joke, failing to see Jenny blanch at the suggestion of sleeping with an older man. The correlation to her own situation was a little too close, and it made her certain that she'd made the right choice. Her desire for Andrew confused her. She felt almost guilty wanting him so much, and unexpectedly disloyal to David for enjoying his attention. Every second was burned into her mind and even now, her body ached to feel his lips again. She lashed out at Karen for saying things that only made her feel more faithless and guilt-ridden.

"Karen, what would Danny say if he heard you? I swear, if I didn't know you, I'd think you were a tramp. You are lucky to have a man like him! That you would even *look* at another man, much less suggest all the lewd things you'd do if you were me, or if you were single," Jenny's caustic tone was accompanied by sarcastic air quotes. "if I had David back, I wouldn't even *think* of another man in a thousand years." Jenny stomped back to her room and slammed the door. It wasn't Karen's fault that she had Danny, and Jenny knew she loved him. Karen had always been outrageous and attacking her for it wasn't fair. But right now, after her kiss with Andrew, Jenny was shaken and needed a target.

Karen was speechless. She couldn't remember the last time she and Jenny had had harsh words for each other. She was hurt. But so, obviously, was Jenny. Jenny was right though, she was lucky to have a man like her Danny. She would go home and hug him, and he would be there for her, just as he always was. Poor Jenny.

Chapter 13

Jenny found herself making the trek to see David more and more often. It seemed she'd been to David's graveside every day this week, trying to remember him, and begging him to send her her next great love. As if he could do anything for her from Heaven. She had gone weekly for the first couple years, and then every couple weeks, and then, this spring she'd stopped going. But she needed someone to talk to again. She couldn't talk to Karen. Karen didn't seem to understand that she wasn't looking for a casual fling, she wanted a husband. Andrew couldn't be that for her, and she wasn't going to get her heart broken when he decided he'd had enough of the old lady.

However much she wanted to protect her heart, though, she missed her friend more. Perhaps she should talk again to Andrew. Surely he would understand and want to be her friend again. If only she could explain to herself why he was so important, maybe she could explain it to him, too.

Jenny was ill, that could be the only explanation, thought Karen. She wasn't eating anymore, the sparkle had gone out of her eyes again. Or, maybe it was time to corner Andrew. Karen had been so sure there was a blossoming romance there. If Jenny wouldn't talk, though, Andrew was the only other one who might know what was going on. Karen called him with the pretense that her faucet wasn't working again, and he met her right after work that afternoon.

"Andrew, tell me about Jenny. Do you know what's going on with her? She won't talk to me, and frankly I'm worried. I thought…is there something going on with you two? She's never mentioned you as a love interest, but I'm not blind. She glows anytime she sees you; if you come up in conversation, she tries diligently to be nonchalant, and she's not fooling me at all. Tell me what's happened."

"Oh boy, I don't know where to start. Well, I guess at the beginning. Jenny and I have spent a lot of time together this summer. Not just working, but, you know, dinner. Talking. Just keeping each other company. At first, it was innocent enough. She enjoyed mothering me, I think. But then, we became friends, and somewhere along the line everything changed for both of us, I am sure of it. As far as something between us, I think it's only in my mind. I…I'm in love with her, and I don't know why, but she seems to have a real problem with it. I'm too young for her, she says, but I think she loves me. At the very least she cares for me. I know it." Andrew wasn't sure how much more to tell Karen. It was so good to just talk to someone. He was hurt, too, and he didn't know how to talk about this stuff. If the woman was anyone else, he'd call Josh. Obviously he couldn't do that. He sat heavily in the chair closest to him and rubbed both open palms over his face.

Now that she looked closely at him, Karen could see that he looked worn and weary as well. She'd known about the dinners, the gardening, but Jenny had always made it sound very casual, mentioning it in an off-hand way, if at all. Jenny had been hiding him from her, and now things were beginning to make sense. Karen pulled a couple glasses from the cabinet and poured them each an iced tea. She sat across from him and pushed a glass toward him. "Alright, so you love her, she might love you, and you're both miserable. So what happened? Something happened, and she isn't telling me."

"I kissed her. Oh, God… I… I pushed too hard. I kissed her, and when she kissed me back, well, I thought – no, I *didn't* think. Karen, I have waited so long for her. I have been half in love with her since I was sixteen. Back then, I know it was really nothing more than a crush on a fantasy, but I *know* her now. I know her, and I want to be with her. I told her I loved her, and wanted to, you know. Oh, God, she was completely horrified! You should have seen her scramble. Hell, our first kiss and I'm telling her I love her and want to screw her. That's what happened." Andrew couldn't sit still any more. He paced the room while he talked, berating himself yet again for his momentary lack of control. "Jeez! It's not like that. Hell, I'm not a saint, and she's amazing, of *course* I want to… but I mean, I don't *just* want to have sex – I *love* her, for Chrissakes, and I scared her off. I'm sure she thinks I only want... Dammit, I'm such an idiot."

Something Andrew had said a moment ago just clicked with Karen. "Wait, wait, go back. She said what? She thinks you're too young? Oh, holy hell. I'm afraid I didn't help your cause then. What day was this? I went over to Jen's on Saturday and teased her about having dinner for two the night before. That was the night you were over? I mentioned old Ben the grocer. He has been making passes at her for years, and he's old enough to be her dad. I know she made a comparison. Dammit! That isn't what I meant at all. He's not you, and it's completely different! Ben wants a hook-up. You love each other. I am certain she loves you, even if she hasn't told me so. No one is this unhappy if her heart isn't seriously engaged. Oh, Andrew. We need to fix this. She needs to give you a chance. Don't you worry. We're going to straighten this out. I promise." Karen only hoped she could deliver on this one.

They were sitting in the park, lunch finished, but lunch hour not over. Karen decided to just jump in with both feet, tact be-damned.

"Jen, have you ever thought of looking, I dunno, for a non-traditional partner? You know, someone unexpected like Andrew, for instance. He's a little younger, but…"

"No."

"No? You haven't even thought about it? He's sweet and --"

"No, Karen. Drop it, okay?"

Karen dropped it. *Wow, that touched a nerve.*

The sun was setting over the hill where Jenny rested beside David's headstone. She continued her imagined conversation with him, and could almost hear his voice commenting on her meandering thoughts. *Joshie's moving – Houston. Can you believe it? Oh, but he's going to love it there, I know. And I'll get to visit. You know I always wanted to see Texas, and now I have a reason to go. Emily called the other day to talk to me! I love her. You would love her. She's sweet and wonderful for him...*

Jenny rambled on about the boys and Karen and anything she could think of. She'd long ago kicked the habit of informing David of everything that was going on, as though he were out of town for a while, and needed to be kept abreast for when he returned. But today she needed David's ear. Jenny was glad it was near dark. She shuddered to think what people would say if they saw her lying in the grass next to David's headstone. She wanted to be comfortable, and she'd always loved lying on the ground. It was comforting to stare at the sky, whether it was filled with stars or fluffy clouds. It made her feel young again, even if just for a few minutes.

She finally brought up the subject that had been weighing on her all day. *Even Karen thinks I should see him, can you imagine? I don't know what she's thinking. She's high on something, I'm telling you. Maybe she thinks I'm just gonna jump him a couple times and get him out of my system, then look for real. You know I don't do that. Ugh, no, to be honest, I* really *think she has this crazy romantic notion that he's my True Love, if only I'd give in to it. But, David… He… I…*

Ugh, I miss you! Why can't it just be the way it was? Jenny stopped her stream of conversation for a moment to formulate her next thoughts. It's not that she really wanted to go back, she just wanted things to be easier. She thumped her palms on the ground in frustration. *I want… Dammit, I want Andrew. I* like *him! He gets me, just like you did. But David, I'm so old compared to him! If he were even a few years older, maybe.* She covered her face with her hands in embarrassment, as if she could hide from her thoughts. *But I…I don't want him to see me get old. Isn't that awful? You know how vain I can be.*

Jenny rolled her eyes and smiled, thinking of all the times he'd teased her about it, too. *I never even gave it a second thought with you. We were going to get old together! And seriously, who thinks about the reality of getting older when they're nineteen? Not me! I thought we'd just go on forever! Dammit, David, I'm still mad at you for leaving me!* Her tone softened. *And I love you. Help me get through this, okay? There's gotta be a better match for me. Find me a good one. Love you, Sugarbear.*

Jenny stood up and shook out the blanket she'd brought and headed back home.

Chapter 14

Karen popped into Jenny's office just before they left for the day, hoping she'd catch Jenny in a good mood, or at least an agreeable mood. "Jenny? Mark Adama came in today. He's having a get together at the pub. I thought…well, Danny and I are going. Do you want us to pick you up? You need to get out, Sweetie. It'll do you good." Karen felt like she was walking on eggshells this week. She had for the past two weeks, really. The life had drained out of Jenny after the incident with Andrew. Karen had no idea how to help her friend. She wouldn't talk about Andrew, didn't want to even admit there was anything wrong, or that something had happened with him. It made it hard for Karen to broach the subject if Jen insisted there was no subject to be broached. And as far as her promise to Andrew, Karen felt more and more discouraged that she'd be able to keep it. Her only hope at the moment was to force them to share space. She was pretty certain he'd be there, too. Surely, if Jenny saw him...

"Sure, Karen, I guess. This isn't a ploy to set me up, is it? I'm done dating. I'm going to take a break, okay?"

"I promise. There's no one. Just friends getting together for drinks. Mark and his wife are having a party while some friend is in town, that's all." *And if Andrew is there, he's just another 'friend', right?*

Jenny dressed deliberately in her yellow sundress. If she couldn't quite feel sunny, at least she could look it. Perhaps it would rub off on her until she was as perky as the dress. She was determined to enjoy this evening. Karen was right. It would do her good to get out. No more moping.

The local pub was alive with sound as Karen, Danny and Jenny made their way through the door. Karen led the way, forging a path straight to the covered patio behind the bar. It was the best place in town for gatherings, with plenty of seating, a festive atmosphere, and good food and drink. She found a corner table to drop her wrap on, thus reserving it for their use. Karen took charge of everything immediately, sending Danny off to fetch drinks.

"Jen, you look super." Karen exclaimed. "I'm so glad you wore the yellow dress. You look so perky." Glancing toward the door, she spied Andrew making his way in. Danny was right behind him with drinks in hand, talking over his shoulder to someone. *Oh, my, he is handsome! And Andrew isn't so bad, either.* She smiled to herself. Some people wondered not-so-subtly what she and Danny saw in each other. They seemed so opposite. But he was her complement, her other half, and he was a damn fine looker, if she did say so herself.

Danny approached them with a smile. "Look who I found at the bar? Jenny, I know you know Mark. Please let me introduce you to his good friend Robert Campbell. He's in town for a couple months. And here's your wine. You must take a sip first, let me know if it's the right one." He winked at her and handed over the glass of liquid courage. He may not approve of all his wife's matchmaking shenanigans, but he adored Jenny, and he, too, wanted her to be happy.

"Thank you, Danny." She took a quick sip of the sweet wine she preferred. "Perfect!" She smiled at him and turned to meet this Robert. Jenny was struck dumb. He was like a man out of an old movie. Tall, dark, handsome, elegant, she only hoped her jaw wasn't hanging open. She had the distinct feeling it was.

"I am pleased to meet you, Jenny." Robert took her offered hand and raised it to his lips, placed a kiss on her fingertips, and lowered it again. "Danny tells us you work at the library with the lovely Karen?" He turned his attention to Karen and greeted her also with an old-fashioned kiss to the hand. Jenny and Karen were both stunned silent. Who does that anymore? Robert, though, pulled it off, with sincerity and polish. No one else they knew could do that without evoking giggles from the recipient!

"Oh, yes – yes, I'm pleased to meet you as well!" She smiled with charm, hoping it would cover her surprise. That was all Jenny could think to say, letting it suffice for the moment.

Karen found her voice. "New to town, then? I want you to meet a few people. I know you will feel at home here in no time." They moved away from the group and made small talk and introductions around the room. The gathering may have been intended as small, but as the pub got more crowded, people filtered out onto the patio, and more introductions were made. Robert was a good sport and allowed Karen to take charge of him, but his eyes often wandered to the woman he'd first been introduced to, Jenny. She was lovely, and Robert wanted a few minutes more with her. If only there weren't so many people here tonight!

"Karen, sweet lady, I beg of you, have mercy on me! I'm parched. Do you mind if we sit for a moment and have a nice glass of wine?" He chuckled and took her arm in his own, guiding Karen back to the table in the corner. Danny, lucky dog, was lounging in the back, feet extended and glass of wine propped on the arm of his chair. "Danny, you strike me as quite a genius, ordering bottles of wine for the table and glasses, too. Brilliant." Robert proceeded to pour a glass for himself and was just lowering himself into a seat when Jenny glided back over. He stood and offered her the glass. "Wine? Only just poured and still chilled."

"Why, thank you! I believe I will! Oh, Karen, how do you manage it? All these people, and you seem to know every one!" Jenny sat in the nearest available chair and took a long sip of the cool wine. "I'm exhausted already. Robert, how many people has she introduced you to? I'm sure there will be a quiz later, so I hope you remember all their names!" Jenny giggled and smiled up at Karen. It may have been the wine on an empty stomach, but Jenny was feeling beautiful and flirty, and it seemed too good to be true that there was a handsome man right here to flirt with. Robert something. Mr. Wonderful.

"Ah, yes, I remember most everyone, but I am definitely not ready for a quiz!" Robert was mesmerized by her smile and her laugh and he wondered if she was here alone. He was positive he'd not been introduced to another Martin, and she wore no wedding band. Perhaps she was here with a companion. As if on cue, he noticed her eyes lock onto someone across the room. Her smile froze for just a split second, and her cheeks heated before the color drained. She took another long sip of wine and turned to him, a determined sparkle in her eyes. He didn't have to see who it was to know that even if she was here alone, she wasn't entirely available. But then again, neither was she entirely taken. Either way, she was a beautiful woman, he was single, and two months was a long time to sleep alone.

"Oh, no, thank you. I can see myself home, but you are very kind to offer, Robert." Jenny was ready to be alone, and a silent walk home in the moonlight would be a pleasure. Karen had been right. It had been very good to be out tonight. And she'd met Robert. He didn't seem too keen on her walking home alone, but he was at least smart enough not to push the issue with her. Just when she'd given up on dating, she'd met Mr. Wonderful. Life was so funny.

Jenny wrapped her shawl over her shoulders and removed her sandals, swinging them loosely at her side as she strolled the few blocks home. She thought over her time with Robert. He'd been an engaging conversationalist, witty and charming. He'd even laughed at her jokes, something none of the other men had done, at least, not sincerely. She'd thought he would ask her to dinner, but he hadn't. Perhaps he would, though. She rather hoped he would. Robert was just the sort of man every girl dreamed of. He was just the sort of man who might help her forget…

Unbidden, a picture of Andrew came to mind. Andrew, as he'd been the night they'd kissed. All brawny male, breath ragged with need, eyes burning with want…warm lips and hands…she couldn't forget, didn't want to forget, even though the remembering made her feel wretched. She'd seen him tonight and had known he was there almost from the moment he'd arrived. At one point, he'd caught her eye and started toward her, but she'd quickly focused her attention on Robert, and the next time she'd looked, Andrew was nowhere to be found. And now she wished she hadn't cut him off. She missed him. It would have been nice to talk to him again.

Andrew sat on the patio under the pergola he'd built for her. He could smell the roses and honeysuckle on the trellises, warm summer scents that he'd come to associate with Jenny. How many times had they sat here after dinner, enjoying the deepening night, a glass of iced tea or a beer in hand, heads tilted back on the edge of their chairs to see the stars? Talking about anything and nothing, or not talking at all? He missed her. It was past time to ask forgiveness, to put his bad behavior behind them and try to start again. He would wait here until morning if he had to. He only hoped she came home alone, not knowing quite what he'd do if Robert brought her home. Luckily, he didn't have long to wait, nor did he have to deal with Robert. In the light of the bright full moon he saw her amble up the driveway and he stood. Her shoes were in her hand, and she looked the picture of female insouciance. How like her – she loved her shoes, but she loved to feel the earth beneath her soles as well. The best of both worlds, she'd say.

"Warm hands, cold heart, dirty feet and no sweetheart. You should keep your sandals on at least until you get home, you know. Who knows what you could've stepped on in the dark, especially with no one to carry you home." Andrew hoped his teasing tone would put her at ease. It was so natural to use it with her. She brought out his playfulness like no one else did.

Jenny's mouth curved in a smile as she recognized the voice and the figure standing at her door. "Andrew. I was just thinking of you. I'm so glad you're here. I'm sorry we didn't talk at the pub. I shouldn't have ignored you like that." She continued her slow amble until she stood directly in front of him.

"No, no, I deserved it. Besides, you were enjoying the company, and it was easier to leave and meet you here anyway." As she drew closer all the words he'd practiced seemed to vanish. The debonair chap he wanted to be disappeared, too, and, though he'd rehearsed apologies for the past hour, nothing seemed to be left in his brain.

"I owe you an apology." He stared at her as he tried to think of something clever to say. Her gaze was unwavering, if a bit questioning. *Where are those fancy phrases?* He blurted the first thing he could think of. "I'm sorry. I'm sorry I kissed you, and I'm sorry I propositioned you, and I'm sorry we don't talk anymore. I'm sorry I was mad. I'm sorry if I hurt you. I'm sorry. I miss you." He did not apologize for telling her he loved her. He wouldn't be sorry for that.

Jenny stared at him, uncertain what to do. The last thing she'd expected was an apology. He was *sorry? Oh…* She reached for him, touching his arm lightly. "Sweetheart…I'm sorry, too. I've missed you, too." She dropped her shoes into the chair beside her and reached her arms out in an unspoken request for a hug. "Friends?"

Andrew was beginning to hate that word, but took her into his arms. If she was so determined to maintain friendship, he would cherish his friend. "Friends." He did his best not to crush her, keeping the embrace as friendly and short as he could. "Now, my dear *friend*, tell me how you enjoyed your evening." The teasing tone was back, even if the smile didn't quite make it to his eyes.

"Oh dear, yes. I had a fine time. I met the most dashing gentleman. I thought he might ask for my number, but he didn't. Do you think he will? You'll tell me if you don't think he's right for me? I don't want to waste my time anymore. Does he have potential?"

Andrew wondered if she was as unaffected by his embrace as she seemed. *How could she so casually mention another man, ask me these questions?* Perhaps he'd imagined the shiver, the quick intake of breath, or maybe she was just cold.

"Hmmm...potential? Yes, I suppose so. He'd be an idiot not to ask you out." Unfortunately, he *did* seem suited to her. Andrew wouldn't lie, even to give himself the upper hand. It was clear that she wanted – or *thought* she wanted – someone older. If that's what she thought she wanted then that's what she'd have. Until she realized that she was his. And if she didn't, well he'd cross that bridge when he got to it.

Karen popped over with a conspiratorial gleam in her eye. "He's on the phone. Line two. I told you he'd call. Say yes."

Jenny rolled her eyes. Of course she'd say yes. She answered as calmly as she could. "This is Jenny."

Robert wasted no time beating around the bush, but asked her for dinner the next evening. He was definitely no-nonsense and businesslike on the phone. But she could hear his smile as she agreed and they made arrangements. Dinner on Wednesday at a quiet little bistro. He'd pick her up at seven. Robert was definitely not used to the country hours she kept.

"Alright, Karen, I said yes. Now help me decide what to wear." Jenny was looking forward to the week a great deal more than she had been ten minutes ago. She felt like a teenager going on her first real date!

Jenny sat in her front room, staring at a photo of her with David, taken on their honeymoon. She was so young – *they* were so young! Everyone said they were crazy to get married straight out of high school. They were right. It was crazy, and it hadn't been easy. She'd been a mother before she'd finished her sophomore year of college. But they'd made it work. They'd fought hard for the life they had, and it had been an amazing twenty-five years.

Jenny stared hard at the girl in the photo, tracing her features as though trying to reconcile the girl she'd been with the woman she was now. That girl had been fearless, blissfully unaware that heartbreak was in her future. Now, Jenny was reserved, careful, and very much afraid of heartache. She wanted to be more like that girl in the photo. Open and free, fearless of heartache. After all, now she knew the worst of it and had come out stronger on the other side, hadn't she? Would she trade a moment with David to save herself from losing him? Of course not.

Jenny, you can be that girl, and she's in here somewhere. Be brave and fearless! Go for it!

Jenny knew she was supposed to be suitably impressed. Robert was a fascinating man. She fleetingly wondered what he was doing here in small-town America. He belonged in New York City or Paris. Somewhere cosmopolitan, that's for sure. He was the ideal gentleman. He'd opened doors for her, held her chair as she was seated for dinner, even stood when she excused herself. Polite at every turn.

She was duly impressed with his manners, his conversation, and his tall, dark, handsome features. Robert was perfect. *If only… If only he had a mischievous gleam in his eye when he spoke. Or deep dimples when he smiled. If only he made my heart flutter.*

"Karen, I promised to call. I'm calling." Jenny sounded dejected, even to herself. She couldn't help it, and Karen was surely the only one she could talk to about this. Her dinner with Robert had been wonderful. It was almost perfect. Perhaps Karen could explain, then, why she was feeling so underwhelmed.

"Jenny, dear, you are supposed to be giggly and gushy and girly. You sound…you sound disappointed. You did go, didn't you? Tell me."

"It was good, very good. We had a lovely dinner, and we seem to have things in common. Lots of talking and no awkward silence… I don't know. It was good. But shouldn't I be giddy? I don't know why I'm not giddy. He was lovely, really, and I did say I'd love to meet again…"

Karen cut to the chase. "Did you kiss him? Or rather, did he kiss you?"

"That's the strange part. I was sure he was going to kiss me. You know that look. But then he didn't. I thought he would, and... Karen, he shook my hand! He didn't even kiss it!" Maybe that was what was leaving her depressed. She'd thought the date had gone well enough, and he hadn't even been attracted enough to kiss her hand? Depressing, indeed.

"Oh, Sweetie, some guys just save it. You know, waiting for the perfect moment. He's been a gentle-man so far, and he does seem a little old-fashioned, you have to admit."

"You're right. Of course you're right. I'm sure it's fine. We'll go out to dinner again, and it will be wonderful, and he'll sweep me off my feet and take me to live in the castle I'm sure he has tucked away somewhere." Jenny felt much better and was able to laugh at the thought of anyone sweeping her off to a castle, especially Mr. Wonderful!

"Look at me! I've been doing all the talking, and I'm quite sure you've heard enough about my sons to hold you for weeks. Tell me about you." There were any number of things Jenny wanted to know about Robert, first and foremost, how a catch as remarkable as him wasn't already married. He was handsome, charming, intelligent, and, most endearing to her, a bit shy.

"Well, what do you want to know? My job would bore you, lots of number crunching and staring at charts for hours, not glamorous at all. You know I'm from Chicago. And I don't have much family to speak of, though I love hearing about yours!" Robert figured she wanted to know what every woman wanted to know – why wasn't he married? And was there a chance for her to be the future Mrs. Campbell? He was used to the chase, both as hunter and hunted, and it was a game he was adept at playing, although it grew ever more tiresome.

Jenny knew a diversionary tactic when she heard one. Jenny grew serious for just a moment, and stared intently, debating whether to ask or not. Her voice was quiet as she voiced her thought.

"Sometime, I want you to tell me about the one that got away. Who broke your heart so?" Her eyes searched his for a moment before she smiled and changed the subject. "But for now, I want the most audacious story you can remember about you and Mark from college. I want something I can taunt him with at their Christmas party when everyone is tipsy and telling stories on each other."

Robert was taken aback. Sure, he was rather used to women wanting to mend his broken heart. Why they all assumed he must be nursing one, he'd never know. But Jenny had seemed to see inside him just now. As though she knew the story and was only waiting for his version of it. It was strange, and it made him slightly uncomfortable, but then she'd changed the topic, and the moment was transformed. He smiled in return and leaned forward to tell her the juiciest tidbit fit for mixed company.

"Thank you for dinner, Robert. I had a lovely time." She smiled up at him as she spoke. She had enjoyed this time much more than the last. He had opened up to her a little, and both of them had been more relaxed. There was a twinkle in his eye as he related anecdotes of college follies with Mark, and though he didn't have dimples, he still had a lovely smile. And once, she'd caught him looking at her with an intensity that had made her heart skip. It had been wonderful.

She truly *had* enjoyed herself. And she hoped, as they walked through her gate, that he would kiss her this time.

"I am sure the pleasure was all mine. You are delightful, Jenny." Robert slowed as they reached her door, and turned to look at her. She shone in a sweet pink dress. On any other woman her age, the dress would have been too girlish, but Jenny looked just right. Demure yet sexy. Vibrant. He took her hand and caressed its back with his thumb. "I'd like to see you again." He smiled warmly as he spoke, confident she'd say yes, looking forward to another dinner, perhaps a museum, too, next time. And to getting to know her better.

She smiled right back at him. "I'd like that very much." She glanced down at his lips, hoping he'd take the hint. Her free hand swept an imaginary tendril behind her ear. Robert didn't disappoint. He leaned down and brushed his lips over hers. Jenny tilted her chin up and stepped closer, inviting a more lingering kiss. She felt his tongue trace the seam of her lips, tentatively, testing her. She wanted to be *kissed* – had been obsessed with it since their last date – she wanted to see if she reacted with him as she had with Andrew. Unfair to them both, perhaps, but she needed to know. She opened slightly, leaned in a bit more.

Oh, Dear Lord, she is tempting. Robert was hard-pressed to keep the kiss light and simple. He had been celibate for too long, and her enticing kiss pulled at him. If she asked him in, he wasn't sure he'd say no. She was not ready to fall into bed with him just yet, and he wanted that more than anything. It was the reason he hadn't kissed her last time. Robert wanted her to feel she was the one doing the seducing. Though, perhaps if he was honest, it was nice to feel he wasn't prey or predator, only a desired companion. He broke the contact and pulled away, a chagrined chuckle breaking the silence. His eyes roved over her face, her sweet eyes looking back up at him. He met her gaze and took a chance.

"Jenny, you are enchanting. Please, I'd like to take you out again Saturday. I have something in mind I think you'd really enjoy. Do you like Italian?"

Chapter 15

Andrew was under a desk, of all things, when he heard Robert and Mark chatting in the hall. He knew he shouldn't be listening as soon as Jenny's name came up, but there was no way to avoid it.

"The plane will be ready at the airport at noon. A quick hop over to Chicago, take in a couple sights, stop in at the apartment for a change of clothes, and we'll be seated for dinner at seven. Taking her to Mamma Luisa's. Then we can either hop back, or I'm rather hoping she wants to see the apartment more closely. I've had the housekeeper freshen it up, just in case."

"Well, I know the women love you, Robert, but I'm telling you, small-town girls take a lot more wooing."

"And I'm telling you, she wants it. She may not realize it yet, but she's on a slow burn, and I intend to set her completely on fire. You should have seen her practically begging me to kiss her last night. Once she gets another taste, she'd going to be ravenous." Robert knew he sounded like a cad, but he had his pride. Better to act the cad he'd always been than for Mark to suspect that he might finally be hooked himself.

"She's not your average woman, Robert. She's a real lady. You're rushing your fences with this one. But I won't tell you how to run your life." Mark's voice trailed off as they moved away from the door.

Holy hell…Jenny isn't going to like this one bit. Andrew suddenly found that he didn't like Robert so much after all. If he were a violent person, he might have to do damage to that damned perfect face. There was no way in hell he was telling her. She wouldn't believe him, and she'd likely shoot the messenger.

"Karen, Karen! Get over here. Right. Now." Jenny's barely contained whisper was demanding. Karen moseyed over to Jenny's office and lounged at the door.

"Yes? Did you have something to tell me?" She knew it had to be something to do with Robert. She said he'd kissed her after the last date, short and sweet, but very nice! And he'd asked her out for tomorrow.

"Karen, you will not believe this! Just got off the phone with Robert. He is picking me up early tomorrow and we'll be gone all day. I'm supposed to dress for walking, and bring something fancy to change into. What does it mean?" Jenny's excitement was barely contained. She couldn't think where they could possibly go. The big cities were several hours' drive, and where would she change? "You have to help me! I have no idea what to wear and what to take. Help!"

"Sounds like you might want to take your toothbrush, too." Karen muttered under her breath, but Jenny heard it anyway.

"Don't be silly. He's been a perfect gentleman! I'm sure he doesn't have any such thought, at least, not *yet*! But maybe someday," she sighed. "He's awfully handsome! And his kiss was tantalizingly short. I need to gather more information." Jenny grinned. She'd told Karen about the too-brief kiss, and that she was dying to kiss him again. He was altogether too shy in the romance department, which struck her as amusing, since he seemed so cosmopolitan and debonair in every other respect. Jenny quite liked him so far, and in the spirit of fearlessness, she was taking a chance, and pursuing a relationship with him. He seemed very much like the answer to all her prayers.

"I don't know. No hints? He didn't say anything else?" Karen's radar was up. She liked Robert, liked him just fine, but this didn't sound like an average afternoon out. It sounded suspiciously like a Grand Gesture, meant to sweep Jenny right off her feet. Tumbling her right into bed, more like. Jenny might be a widow, but she was still innocent. She wouldn't know what hit her. That made her vulnerable and sent Karen's protective instinct into overdrive. She'd find out what all this was about, and soon. Mark was only a phone call away, and she'd wrangle it out of him if she had to. Karen left Jenny thinking of the date at hand while she went to make that phone call to Mark.

Karen hung up the phone and stared intently at the receiver, as if it would explain more clearly the conversation she'd just had with Mark. *Well, Hell's Bells. Jenny is going to flip – a day trip to Chicago?* Karen didn't know quite what to think, and Mark was as vague on the one hand as he was helpful on the other. There was definitely something odd about this. *Swept off her feet, indeed…*

"Andrew, I'm too excited to work. Help me pick something to wear tomorrow. Karen's been no help at all!" Jenny called over to him from the front porch.

"Seriously? I am not helping you dress for a date. That's what girlfriends do. Sorry, Charlie." Andrew wasn't about to help for tomorrow. For one thing, he wanted her for himself, and she knew it, or ought to know it, if she weren't too stubborn to see it. And for another, he dreaded even the mention of tomorrow. He knew what Robert had in mind. He should tell her, but how could he? Admit that he'd been eavesdropping? Or disappoint her hopes in Perfect Robert. He knew she liked Robert, and really, he was a nice guy, even though he was a little warped about relationships and women.

He could see from the garden how Jenny's face fell when he'd told her no. "Oh, now stop that. You know I can't help with that stuff. You look good in everything. Just pick something." He couldn't bear to see her hurt, even if she had no business asking him this favor.

"Alright, I'll pick. But will you just look and see what you think? Just a quick look-see, that's all! I promise, no fashion show!" Tomorrow sounded special, and she wanted to look just right.

"Jenny… ugh. Alright. But you owe me a beer. This is *not* guy-friend territory." Against his better judgment, he got cleaned up and went inside to see what she had in mind. *Lord, just kill me now. I'm helping her pick out freaking dresses.*

Andrew was cracking open what was sure to be the first of several beers when Jenny waltzed into the kitchen wearing a black dress. The dress fit her to perfection, emphasizing each and every tantalizing curve. She looked stunning. Her hair, usually up in a simple ponytail, curled in soft layers around her jaw and neck and shoulders. She'd removed her jewelry and her feet were bare. Her eyes shone with nervous expectation, and her lush lips curved in a half-smile as she presented herself for his approval.

"What about this? Do I look okay? Do you think this will work for both a day walking about, and an evening dinner or something?" Jenny looked at Andrew's slack jaw and glazed eyes, waiting as the silence stretched into awkwardness for her. "Andrew? Say something." She began to fidget with the skirt, uncertain now of her choice. She'd thought it such lovely dress when she bought it, but she guessed from his silence that he didn't want to hurt her feelings. In a small voice, she stated, "You don't like it. I thought…"

"Jenny…" Andrew had to clear his throat, for his voice had gone raspy with a need he was trying to control. "Jenny, you look stunning. Really. This Robert, you like him…" It wasn't a question, and he didn't want an answer. He strode to the window and stared at the trellis.

"Yeah, I really like him. Not just that, but he's like an answer to all my hopes. I want what I had with David, and I won't settle for less. What if Robert is the one? I need to take a chance!" Jenny had advanced on him, was near to touching his waist when he turned around.

Andrew's heart ached, his mind reeling. *What if Robert is the one? Why can't* I *be the one?* He was sure the hurt showed in his eyes, but he didn't care anymore. He was tired of hiding his feelings out of consideration for hers. She was closer than he'd realized. *Close enough to touch.* He lifted his fingers to her face and traced over her cheek ever so lightly.

"You are beautiful, do you know that?" His voice was barely a whisper. He pushed a tendril behind her ear, and traced it with the gentlest touch. *Close enough to kiss.* He closed the gap between them and rested his forehead against hers. "Jenny…" He touched his lips to her cheek. "Any man will be lucky to have you. If Robert has any sense at all, he'll fall at your feet and worship you. You are…" He no longer trusted his voice. He had so much to say, yet, he couldn't. She had no intention of considering him, and Andrew was tired of waiting. Tired of being "just friends" in hopes that someday they'd be more. He couldn't begin to compete with a dead husband, and now it seemed he was losing her to a man she barely knew. Andrew walked to the door and let himself out. He couldn't bear to spend another moment with her. With her so close, yet, not his. Never his. He walked himself home, going straight to bed.

Jenny stood staring at the door, hands pressed against her cheeks, trying to cool the heat that had rushed to them at his touch. He'd left so abruptly, she hadn't had time to register that he had kissed her. As though he were saying goodbye. She had the sinking feeling she had just made a terrible mistake.

She locked the door and slowly made her way to her room, turning out the lights as she went. She undressed at her bedside in the late evening glow, reliving the single moment Andrew had touched her and kissed her face, wishing she could call him back to her side.

Chapter 16

Robert rang her doorbell at precisely 11:30 and drove her to the little municipal airport outside of town. *This is going to be a strange day. Plane watching, maybe?* Jenny was slow to realize that they were going to be on a plane. *One of those little tiny planes…*

"Robert? Can I ask yet what our plans are?" If he'd been less preoccupied with talking to the pilot about the preflight inspection, he'd have noticed the fear creeping into her voice. She'd flown before, and even enjoyed it, but it had been a large commercial jet. Not one of these little four-seaters.

Robert glanced over to her and smiled. "I thought I'd take you to my hometown, show you around a bit." Another smile and a wink, and he was back to the pilot.

Jenny, remember: Fearless. You can do this. It must be safe, or he wouldn't be taking you. It's going to be fine. Just fine…

Once they were up in the air, he began a running monologue about Chicago, for that's where they were heading, and Millennium Park, which is where they'd be spending the afternoon, as well as Mamma Luisa's, his favorite Italian restaurant. She peppered him with questions, for she was truly interested, especially if they were going to further their relationship. But she found that she wasn't feeling so well. He seemed so excited to show her his city that Jenny hoped she'd feel better once they got on the ground.

Her head was beginning to pound. She'd been so nervous this morning, coupled with fretting over Andrew last night, Jenny realized that she hadn't eaten yet today. At least she'd had her coffee. It was something, but between lack of food, her nerves, and the blinding sunshine flooding the cabin, today was not getting off to a good start. Jenny turned her attention back to Robert. If she just kept her focus on him, maybe her head would calm down.

Robert had a driver waiting for them in Chicago – a driver! Who was this man? He was much more than she'd originally thought. Yes, she'd known he was a successful businessman, and a long-time friend of Mark's, but having a chauffeur in Chicago? And to fly her here, just for the day? Jenny was unsure what to think and she was hesitant to ask. She didn't want to seem awed or overwhelmed, or worse, like a gold digger! Besides, she had bigger issues on her mind. Like the fact that her headache had only grown worse over the course of the two-hour flight, and now she was sick to her stomach. She needed to eat, and couldn't wait until dinner.

"Robert, do you mind if we stop for a bite somewhere? Something simple is fine. I just need to get some food in my system. I'm not feeling so well…"

Robert looked at her for the first time – really looked at her. "Oh, Jenny! Why didn't you say something?" He felt like such an ass, prosing on and on about the wonders that were in Chicago, that he didn't even notice she'd been slowly turning green. She looked awful, really, but of course he knew better than to say so.

Robert instructed the driver to take them to his apartment instead. Jenny was in no condition to be walking all over the park in the hot sun. It was certainly not how he'd planned to spend the day, but maybe after a bit she'd feel up to dinner.

They walked sedately through the building, and he opened the door for her, pointing out the small powder room just to one side of the entrance. She was inside, with the door slammed shut in a second. Robert could hear her retching. *Good Lord…* He hurried to the kitchen to grab a cool glass of water and dampen a hand towel for her.

"Oh, Jenny… You know, I must admit that I'd wanted to show you my place, but this isn't at all the way I'd imagined it." Robert was guiding her to the angular sofa in his modern den. He loved this masculine room, but just now he wished he had a more cozy place to offer her. The only other place to lie down was his bed…

"I'm so sorry – I know you had the day planned and I've ruined it. I am so sorry." Jenny truly was sorry. And mortified. "Maybe after I lie down we can go for dinner? I think I'm feeling better." She wasn't, but she tried to be optimistic. This was a full-blown migraine, and it usually took her a full day to recover. Damn her for forgetting to eat – this was the worst possible way to spend what was supposed to be a grand romantic day.

"Do you want something to eat first? Or something for the headache?"

"No, thank you. I'll take something with the water you gave me, and I don't think I could keep anything else down at the moment. Just let me lie down."

"Alright. If you need anything at all, I'll be in my office, right through that door."

Thirty minutes later he heard the bathroom door again, and dry heaves. This day was a bust. Dammit. He emailed Mark that they'd be staying overnight and why. This was certainly not how he'd meant to get Jenny into bed tonight, but she was miserable, and a trip home would be foolish. They could leave in the morning, after she'd had a good night's sleep.

Robert called softly through the bathroom door again. "Jenny, darling? Are you alright? I brought you more water and another cool cloth. May I come in?"

Jenny spoke through the pain, "I've been better. I'm so sorry Robert, I'll be out in just a second." She hadn't had a migraine in so long she'd forgotten how terrible they were. She flushed the toilet and washed her hands. Glancing at her reflection in the mirror, she hadn't even the energy to be horrified at her appearance. She was sick, and didn't care that handsome, debonair Robert was seeing her at her very worst. She just wanted to lie down and never get up again. Pulling open the door and leaning against the doorjamb, she saw Robert there, glass in one hand and cloth in the other. His eyes were full of concern.

"My dear, I think we'd better rain check dinner, too. I'll tell you what. Let's get you settled into bed, and I'll go downstairs to find you some broth. Luisa is sure to have just the thing. I'll be back before you know it. Don't fret. We'll leave in the morning when you're feeling more yourself."

He led her to his room. She stopped in the door way. "I can't sleep here. This is your room." She couldn't possibly…where would he sleep?

"Yes, it is, but you are more in need of it than I am. I'll use the sofa tonight. It's fine. What sort of gentleman would I be if I let you sleep on the couch in your condition?" His mouth lifted in a half-smile. "And I have something you can wear, if you'd like to change out of your dress. You'll be so much more comfortable." He pulled a soft looking t-shirt from a dresser. "I'll leave you to it, then. And Jenny? I'm sorry, too. But don't worry, I intend to collect on the rain check." He leaned down with a smile and kissed her on the forehead before closing the door behind him.

Jenny knew when she was being managed; she was often the one doing the managing. But just now, she didn't mind. She was grateful for his consideration and tenderness with her. She looked at the shirt in her hand and decided she was just going to go with it. She unzipped her dress and stepped out of it, leaving it to lay on the floor as she pulled the t-shirt over her head and padded to the already-turned-down bed. She slid between the sheets and settled her head gingerly on a pillow. She was profoundly grateful for the dark room, soft linens, and silence. Thank God she'd kept her meds down long enough to get them into her system. She could feel the warm drug-induced lethargy spreading through her limbs and her torso. She finally allowed herself to relax and slip into deep, restorative sleep.

Robert checked on her twice that afternoon and again in the evening before finally giving up hope that she might awaken and want dinner, such as it was. He had long since put her chicken broth into the refrigerator. Jenny must have felt absolutely dreadful. She'd hardly complained, really, and kept apologizing to him as if she could help being sick. This was no ordinary sick, he knew. He was familiar enough with headaches, and she'd had a doozy.

As he tried to find a comfortable position on the couch, Robert thought of Jenny, wearing nothing but his undershirt and comfortably ensconced in his king-sized bed. *Damn…*

Jenny woke slowly, and for a moment couldn't quite remember where she was. Then yesterday came flooding back to her, what she could remember of it. She'd slept away most of the day and all of the night. But as she took stock of her situation, she was relieved to note that she felt like a new woman. Her head felt normal, and her stomach had long since stopped its rebellion. She sat up and looked at the room for the first time. Her dress was draped carefully over a valet chair across from the bed with her shoes and bag placed neatly under it on the floor. The room itself was carefully decorated in dark woods and navy pinstripes, reflecting the proper personality of the man who lived here. How very masculine. And as unlike her airy and feminine room as could be. The door swung slowly open – Robert must be checking on her. He was wearing rumpled clothes from yesterday.

Jenny pulled her knees up to her chest and wrapped her arms around them, making sure she was properly covered, and greeted him shyly, "Good morning, Robert." Surely she needn't be so formal with him, but she was still a bit chagrined at their circumstances. She'd spent the night, he'd seen her in the throes of a migraine, and while they'd not been intimate, there was a certain intimacy to their situation. She wasn't sure what he thought about it all, either, although he'd been very considerate.

"Good morning. Feeling better?" She certainly looked better. The life was back in her eyes, although she was understandably hesitant. "I thought I'd better ask what you want for breakfast. Eggs, perhaps, or toast? I don't have too much. I picked up a couple things while I was out yesterday. There is broth, too, if you want it."

"Toast would be lovely, thank you. And perhaps some tea or coffee?" Jenny didn't want a repeat of yesterday. She'd have her breakfast as well as her caffeine fix before they left for home. She'd learned her lesson – no skipping breakfast!

Robert parked his car and went around to open her door. He escorted Jenny to her doorstep with a hand placed gently on the small of her back. He found that after last night he couldn't help but think of Jenny in a more protective light. He'd seen her at her most vulnerable, and she had trusted him to take care of her. She'd had little choice, but he was still touched. He'd held her hand the entire flight home, taking care to reassure her of their safety, and to make sure she didn't have a recurrence of the headache. It wasn't often that he saw this side of women. The women he usually associated with were harder, more self-sufficient, and much less trusting. Mark had been right. She was a different kind of woman altogether, the kind that, perhaps, he could see himself settling down with. It had definitely given him something to think about.

Andrew was just finishing up his morning run when he saw Robert's car pull away from Jenny's house. *Well, screw me…* He felt as though someone had just gutted him. Jenny had done it. She'd stayed with him, with that…*Son of a bitch.* Andrew turned around and headed back to the Reserve. He needed another run to sort out the warring emotions flooding his brain. Andrew couldn't decide whether he'd rather smash Robert's face in, throttle Jenny for falling for whatever line he'd fed her, or throw himself off a bridge and put himself out of his misery once and for all. Another five miles should quiet his mind. He'd be too tired to think by then.

Chapter 17

Jenny called him again, for what seemed like the tenth time this week. Andrew hadn't answered or returned a single phone call or text, nor had he come to the house at all. Jenny was confused and hurt. At the very least, he could tell her what was so wrong, why he wouldn't talk to her. It couldn't possibly be Robert. He'd given Robert his seal of approval. *Yet…* She hated to think of that last evening, when Andrew had all but said goodbye with his kiss. If only she'd known how final that was, she would never have let him go. She had her own pride, though, and she wouldn't seek him out any more. If he wanted her, he knew where to find her.

If Andrew wasn't around, Robert surely was. He was smitten, and spent every spare moment he could with Jenny. After the fiasco trip to Chicago, they had stuck closer to home for their evenings and afternoons out. Robert loved museums and concerts. He seemed to find them everywhere and delighted in sharing them with Jenny. There were few times Jenny could talk him into staying in for an evening, although she could occasionally coax him with the promise of a favorite meal and a good red wine. Jenny would have preferred simpler fare and a good hearty beer, but she enjoyed pleasing Robert. He really was a dream. Cary Grant or Clark Gable couldn't have conjured a more perfect role. If, every now and then, she found herself wishing he was a little more casual, mischievous, or perhaps a little less imposing, she pushed it aside as much as she could.

He was kissing her again. His arms were snaked around her waist and she could feel him pressing against her from behind. She heard his voice, whispering sweet words to her. She leaned into him and lifted her arms to his head, sifting her fingers through his hair as his lips worked their magic, making her want, setting her on fire. When Andrew left her as he always did, she wept in despair.

Jenny and Karen were having lunch. There was nothing unusual in that – they had lunch together almost every day. What was unusual was how chatty Jenny was lately. All she seemed to talk about was 'Robert' this, and 'Robert' that. As glad as Karen was that Jenny seemed to be happy with Robert, she was bothered by how single-minded Jenny's conversation was now. For the past few weeks, Jenny and Robert had been in each other's pockets. She hardly ever saw one without the other. Heck, she almost never saw Jenny outside of work anymore. No hikes in the Reserve, no shopping, no girls' nights. She hated to think that she might be jealous, but it was a distinct possibility. Even Danny had gently chastised her for it.

Then there was Andrew. Poor Andrew. Something had happened while Jenny was in Chicago. Or maybe it was because she had *gone* to Chicago. She wasn't sure what it was, but Andrew was different. He poured himself into his job, working long hours, doing anything and everything he could to work himself to exhaustion.

He had come to the library one day to return a house key. Jenny wasn't there, so he'd given it to Karen with a short note he'd scribbled at her desk. Karen read it, of course. It stated simply that he was unable to continue in her service due to an increased workload elsewhere. That was it. As far as Karen knew, Jenny hadn't seen him since. Karen saw him, though. Karen had let him down, and in a big way. She'd made a promise she'd had no right to make, and that she couldn't keep. The couple of times she'd tried to talk to him about Jenny he'd shut her down quick as lightning, and about as gently. He wanted nothing to do with Jenny, he said. She'd made her choice. Karen tried to ease his broken heart, though, as best she could. She sent all the work she could his way, and hired him herself, mostly so she could keep an eye on him. Between working and running, he was wearing himself to skin and bone. Karen wondered how long he'd punish himself like this before letting go of the grief and pain and, yes, anger. He couldn't go on like this forever.

"I saw Andrew last night at the pub. Drinking alone, I think." Karen had had enough of Jenny's silence on Andrew, and gushing about Mr. Wonderful. She was spitefully pleased to see Jenny blanche before she answered.

"Oh. Did you speak with him? How is he? Haven't seen much of him lately. Tell him I say hello next time you see him. Speaking of Andrew, that reminds me of an idea for a featured book table…" That was the end of that conversation. Karen had the grace to feel momentarily ashamed for her spitefulness, yet, glad to see that Andrew was a weak point. Jenny wasn't entirely heartless when it came to that young man.

Robert and Jenny strolled home from the pub, arm in arm, deep in conversation. They had found a shared love for acoustic live music and frequented the open mic nights, hoping to see their favorite local singers and bands. The gentleman who'd played tonight was their favorite, and they discussed his set list as they walked.

Nearing the door, Jenny slowed and turned to him. It had been a month since they'd started seeing each other. Robert had been patient, always letting her take the lead in their physical relationship, though Jenny was certain that he was occasionally frustrated. Tonight, though, she hoped that perhaps he might help her soothe the ache that had been vexing her all summer. "Robert, will you come in for a bit?" He'd come in for a nightcap many times, but tonight would be different. Her heart pounded in her chest as she opened the door to let them into the kitchen.

"Of course, if you like. You know I will." Robert wondered why she suddenly seemed so skittish. *Could it be? Thank God!* Mark had been absolutely right about her. Although he was sure she was as sexually frustrated as he was, she was hesitant to move beyond kisses. He didn't know what made tonight any different, but if she was willing to go to the next level with him, he didn't care.

Jenny pulled a bottle of white wine from the fridge and set it on the table. Robert placed two goblets next to it, and pulled her close for a kiss.

"Oh..." Jenny melted into his arms and let desire overtake her. She wanted this. Robert's hands were warm and skillful as he pressed her into him, raking his fingers through her locks. She returned his touch with caresses of her own, splaying her fingers over his shoulders and pulling him closer, kneading his muscles as she explored. His lips moved greedily down her neck and his fingers undid the buttons of her jacket and blouse.

"Jenny..." His voice whispered across her skin, setting off shivers of delight. Her eyes drifted closed as she softened still more.

Andrew... Jenny's eyes flew open and she froze in Robert's arms. *Oh please, God, don't let me have said that aloud!*

He felt the change in her immediately and halted his progress. "Jenny? Are you okay? We don't have to do anything you don't want." *Oh, for Chrissakes...*

Jenny was mortified. Reasonably certain that she'd not uttered another man's name, but mortified that she couldn't keep Andrew out of her thoughts anymore.

Jenny pulled away. She wrapped her arms around herself, ashamed, even if he was unaware of the direction her mind had taken. She didn't deserve Robert and his understanding.

"I can't. I'm sorry. I thought… I can't." Jenny's eyes shimmered with unshed tears, and she silently begged him to understand. She dropped her gaze, aware of Robert's barely-contained frustration and the tension in his frame. He might say he understood. He might think he *did* understand. But he didn't like it, and his body language gave him away.

Robert shoved his hands in his pockets and willed his libido to calm down. He took several deep breaths before he trusted himself to speak. "I'll go then. Thank you for a lovely evening. I'll call in the morning if that's okay?" A corner of his lust-riddled mind shouted that he might never call her again if she was going to be such a tease, but Robert pushed the thought aside. She was obviously not ready, and who was he to fault her for being such a devoted wife? Even if her husband had been dead for three years. *Three. Freaking. Years.*

"Yes. Please." Jenny walked to the door and leaned her forehead against it before turning the knob. "Robert, I…I'm sorry." Jenny had no idea what to say. She knew he was trying hard not to be angry, trying to be patient.

He stood at the open door and leaned down to kiss the top of her head. "I'll talk to you tomorrow. Get some sleep." Then he was gone.

She stood against the door for a long time, thinking about what she was supposed to do. Mr. Wonderful was right here, hers for the taking, practically dropped into her lap from heaven. And all her thoughts swirled around a young man who wanted nothing to do with her. *Great. Just great.*

Jenny answered the door with trepidation. She could see Robert on the other side, and she still couldn't decide what to say to him. She wanted so much to be head over heels in love with him. She liked him. Very much. But last night had made it abundantly clear that her feelings for Andrew were not going to be subdued and pushed away.

Jenny greeted him. "Good morning. Come in. Can I get you any coffee? Just made it."

"Thanks. Jenny we need to talk. About last night, and about us." Robert didn't know exactly what to say but the words would come. They always did.

Jenny slowed. She wasn't sure what he wanted to say, but she had a feeling she was about to get dumped. He was pretty upset last night. And who could blame him? "Alright. Let me..." Her voice trailed off as she poured their coffee. Instead of sitting at the table she led him into the living room. She didn't want to be in the kitchen with him, the scene of her latest misstep, and the site of so many memories of Andrew. Even in her own home, she couldn't escape the man.

"Please, sit. Would you like anything else?" Anything to forestall the uncomfortable conversation coming.

"No, nothing, thank you. Please sit with me. I need to talk to you. I only..." Robert took the mug from Jenny's hands and set it on the table, then enveloped her hands in his own. "Jenny," he began. He was certain this was a bad idea, but now that he'd begun, he couldn't let it go. "Darling, there are a few things I want to say to you. Just hear me out, okay?"

"Of course." Jenny's heart raced as she braced herself for his break-up speech. It was more than she deserved. He could have just put a halt to things over the phone. He really was such a lovely gentleman. *Why can't I just love him?*

"I think it was our second date. We were still getting to know each other, and you asked me a not-so-simple question and then proceeded to peer into my soul for a split second. Do you remember that?"

Jenny nodded a slightly confused assent. What did her curiosity about his past matter right now?

"Jenny, you have no idea how many women have asked me that question over the last decade. It gets old after a while, and I've grown cynical. Why women are intrigued, or turned on, by my lack of a Mrs. is a mystery to me. But I've always gotten the same feeling as they ask. The keen interest is unmistakable, and I end up feeling like prey to their predator, some sort of prize to be won. I don't like it, and I inevitably discourage any discussion of the future, especially a future in regards to a new Mrs. Campbell.

But Jenny, for the first time, someone asked me, and I didn't feel like a prize. I felt like a person with a history, someone whose history you actually wanted to know, without having an ulterior motive.

Thank you for that. For seeing *me,* not my marital status, or job, or bank account."

She tried to interrupt. "Robert, I…"

"No, let me finish. Please. I've realized over the past month that your…seeing me has given me hope. So I want to answer that question – perhaps explain myself a little – and hope that you hear me out on some questions I have for you, too."

Jenny didn't answer, but settled deeper into the sofa, tucked her feet under her, and urged him on with a nod. This wasn't at all what she'd expected, and she was extremely curious.

Robert stared at the floor as he gathered his thoughts, and his mind wandered to a place he had tried so hard to forget. "Her name was Debra, and I was about two weeks from asking her to marry me. I had bought the ring, made elaborate plans…and she dumped me. With hardly a by-your-leave, she left me to go back to her old boyfriend. She told me, well, the words hardly matter, but essentially, she said that I was merely a shadow of everything she loved about him. Everything I was, he was *more*.

It sent me into a tailspin, and set me on the path to being who I am today, the me I show the world. I didn't want to be anyone's shadow, so I worked even harder at being a stand-out, the best at everything I put my hand to. Fun-loving Robbie slowly disappeared and was replaced by successful Robert. It has served me well in the business world, and I am good at what I do. I am a man to be reckoned with in a board room, with money and power to back me up. But in my personal life, it has only worked to my detriment. The more successful I became, the more I became a commodity to women, an acquisition to be had, and less a man to partner. And if I'm perfectly honest, I haven't been much better in my treatment of them. Until you."

Jenny's eyes filled with tears. She hurt for him, but he was wrong about her. She wasn't at all the saint he thought she was. She may not have been after his status, but she wasn't much better. She wanted him for all the wrong reasons, too.

"Darling, it's okay. I got over Deb a long time ago, and I know she did me a huge favor. We wouldn't have lasted. But that brings me to what I really wanted to say." Robert inhaled and pushed into his next order of business. "Last night, I came to an uncomfortable conclusion. I'm not used to saying things like this, so please try to hear my intent, if I mess up the words. Last night, when you pushed me away, I realized two things. The first was that I was angry. I had no real right to be so, but I was, and that led me to the second thing. I care. For the first time in forever, I don't *want* to walk away. The old Robert would have shrugged it off and moved on to greener pastures. But now, I care enough not to walk away, and I'm willing to wait until you're ready for whatever happens between us."

"Robert," Jenny tried again to interrupt him, and yet again, he quieted her.

"Jenny, I care for you. Much more than I had intended to the night we met. I'm only in town for a couple months, and I was looking for someone to while away the time with. But you have made me realize that my life needs real change, and real relationship. I hope…I hope that we…that you…"

"Robert, you have to listen to me. I am not what you think I am. And I like you. I really, really *like* you. But I'm not sure..."

"Jenny, I know. I know you're not sure. And the fact that you're telling me makes me even more sure."

"But..."

"Look. I know you're a widow. I know what you had with David was great. But I also know – and have known from the night we met – that there's someone else. I don't know who, and I don't know how serious it is or was, but I know. And I don't care. I'll wait. What's meant to be will be."

Robert really was a dream-come-true. How could he possibly be so understanding? But she'd take what he had to offer. For now. He would be a much better match for her than Andrew, and in time, she'd grow to love him. Surely she would. And if not, he'd given her the perfect out. How could she not at least think about it?

"Robert, can I think about it? I want to love you, and maybe I will in time, but I really need to think over things. You are one in a million, you know that?" Jenny hugged him, squeezing in her own bear-like way, to convey the gratitude she felt for his understanding and kindness.

Jenny turned off her phone. She didn't want to see or talk to anyone. She just wanted to be alone. Well, not entirely alone. She made the long walk to the cemetery and sat on the bench near David's plot. She wanted to be with David. Everything had been so much simpler when he was here. She loved him and he loved her; they had a family, and all was right with the world. Then he'd died. She sat and cried for a long time. Then, when she was finished crying, she fumed. She was angry with him all over again – for leaving her, for destroying their future by leaving her, for making her start over on her own. When she was finished fuming, she cried again. She asked him what to do. She was torn, and worn out, and she wanted nothing more than to have everything back the way it had been with him. *David, I don't know what to do. Help me know what's right – who is right. My gut tells me one thing, my head tells me another. I know you can't help me choose, but I just wish you could send me a sign. I wish I could know that you approve. I trust your level-headed judgment over mine any day. You knew me better than anyone. You would know what to do.*

He saw her there, saw her crying, saw her lovingly caress the top of the headstone before she left. His heart softened for just a moment before he deliberately hardened it again. She had gutted him by choosing Robert. He had been warned; she'd warned him herself. Still, he'd thought she would change her mind. He'd thought that his friendship and love would be enough, but it wasn't. She wanted, hell, he didn't know what she wanted. Someone *older,* that was it. He'd lost her because he wasn't *old* enough. It was enough to make him scream. He didn't think of her as older than him, though she obviously was. She was just Jenny. He felt comfortable with her, he *liked* her, and they were good together. It wasn't enough, though. Robert, that bastard , all he'd had to do was smile his Cary Grant smile and fly her up to Chicago, and she'd fallen right into his bed. It was enough to turn his stomach.

Andrew ran his forearm over his face to wipe away the dripping sweat and continued with his run. He ran until he thought his aching, angry heart would explode, and still it wasn't enough. He thought of her, and wished he could wrap her in his arms, to comfort whatever ache had caused her to weep at her husband's grave. She rejected him, and still, he loved her. He supposed he always would, although it would be nice if the gaping hole in his heart would begin to heal. He turned into the Reserve and walked every mile of trail, exercising his body into exhaustion.

When Jenny got home, she was surprised to find Josh sitting on the patio. She pulled up short. She'd had her phone off all day – what if something was wrong? *What if…* "Josh? What is it? Are you okay? Ryan? Please tell me nothing's wrong!" She rushed to him and grabbed his face, just like she used to, to stare at his eyes. His eyes had always been the giveaway when he was trying to get something past her.

He quietly replied with questions of his own. "Mom, where have you been? Karen was worried and called me. I assured her you were fine, but you did disappear without your phone. It's not like you. So…what's up?" Josh had watched her closely as he spoke, and he could see that she'd been crying recently, even if she thought she could hide it. He engulfed her in a big bear hug. Whatever it was, maybe she'd talk to him. They used to talk a lot, but that was before. He'd grown increasingly distant over the past months, he knew, but he hadn't thought she'd needed him so much anymore. He'd been busy with his impending move and job hunt. He realized that she'd started crying again. "Oh, Mom, what's wrong? Talk to me. It can't possibly be that bad, can it?" He needed answers before his mind created bigger problems.

"Here, we're not going to cry in front of the world. Let's go sit down inside." He walked Jenny into the house and to the sofa, where they could both sit. He kept his arm around her and spoke again. "Tell me. I'm not leaving until you tell me what is so wrong that you're blocking out the people who love you."

"I – I – can't." Her voice was a squeak, and she couldn't articulate everything that weighed on her. How could she explain to him her feelings for Andrew, for Robert? He couldn't possibly understand, and she didn't wish to get into it with him.

"You're not…pregnant…are you?" He was joking, but at her silence… *Oh, God, no!* "Holy Hell, I'm going to have to kill someone – who did this to you?" Josh, usually so mild-mannered, felt a wave of bloodlust flooding his brain. He couldn't sit still. He got up and paced the length of the room furiously until he realized that her quiet sobbing had morphed into laughter. He stopped where he was and muttered, "What's so funny? This is NOT funny."

Jenny tried her best to pull herself together enough to answer. At least she wasn't crying anymore. "You look just like your father, the way you're pacing. He used to do the same thing when he got riled up about something. Joshua, I am *not* pregnant. Don't be so ridiculous. I haven't been with anyone since your father – stop blushing, dear. You brought it up.

If you must know, I was at the cemetery. I miss him so much lately. I know you can understand that." Jenny rose and wandered about the room, trying to decide how much to share with her son. Sure, he was grown, but she was still his mother, and there were certain things boys never wanted to know about their mothers. She picked up one photograph after another. Scattered around the room were the physical reminders of her old life. She had almost no pictures of her new life except one photograph from Ryan's graduation. As she gathered her thoughts, Josh sat again, quiet now, and patient. He'd always been the patient one.

"Remember back in June, how I said that I wanted another chance at love? I know you and your brother were supportive then, but how will you feel when it's real? I think, I think I've found someone but I…" She was holding back tears again.

"Mama," Josh reverted to his little-boy name for her, "Mama, don't you know that Ryan and I want more than anything for you to be happy?" He stood and wrapped her up in his David-like bear hug again. "It'll take some getting used to, but we'll manage. Honest. Has Karen met him? He's going to have to pass muster with Karen and Danny, as well as with Ryan and me. But if you love him, he must be someone special." He kissed the top of her head, just as David had used to do.

How had she managed to raise such a sensitive soul? Josh had known exactly what to say and how to say it. Only he didn't know the half of it. Would he truly be so understanding if he knew everything? Surely, in time they'd get used to the idea. She still didn't know which man truly held her heart. *No, that isn't true at all. You know, you just don't want it to be so…*

"To be honest, there are two men. And I'm torn. One makes all the sense in the world, and I really like him. Karen likes him, too, I know. I could love him, given time. But there is another…" Jenny bowed her head. How could she explain Andrew? And should she? It might be too late, but she still thought of him. She was ashamed to know that she thought of him even when she was with Robert. "I don't know. Maybe there isn't anyone else. It's confusing. I have feelings for someone. I don't think he returns them, at least, not anymore. We… well, I hurt him, and the fact is that I still… Oh, I don't like feeling so mixed up inside! So I went and talked to your dad. I was hoping," Jenny pulled in a ragged breath and let it out in a whoosh. "I was hoping for a sign." Jenny lowered her eyes to the photo in her hand, the picture from their honeymoon. She traced David's face with a fingertip. "It's silly. I know it's silly. But I wish… If I can't have David back, then I wish he would show me what to do."

"I know what you mean." Josh smiled, and gave a short laugh. "I wish Dad could tell me what to do about stuff, too." He wondered who these men were. The second was obviously much more important that she wanted to admit. Maybe he'd stop by Karen's on the way home, if she didn't want to say. He cleared his throat, trying to rid himself of the emotion lodged there. "Will you tell me about them, then?"

"Not just yet. Let me decide what to do first. But, Josh, no matter what happens, please know that I love you and Ryan more than you can imagine. When I introduce another man into our family, you need to remember that. I want you to love him, too. Promise me you'll try."

Josh smiled, "Mom, you worry too much over things." He gave her another squeeze and let her go. "I don't suppose you have any lemonade, do you? Getting all emotional makes a man thirsty, don't you know." And with that, he put an end to the discussion, and led her into the kitchen.

Chapter 18

"Jenny, it's lunch time. Wanna grab something and sit in the park? It's not so hot today – it'll be great!" Karen popped into her office with a smile on her face and purse on her shoulder. Summer was slowly giving way to autumn. The kids had gone back to school and the day-time shift at the library was back to its usual quiet.

"Just a second and I'll be right there." Jenny looked up with a quick grin from the note she was jotting. "Where to, do you think? I'm thinking a deli sub, if that's alright with you." She hadn't had one for a couple weeks, and was hankering for one, especially today.

They headed for their usual spot, chattering about this and that, planning a quick dinner with the men tomorrow evening, an impromptu cookout while the weather was still nice. As they settled in and began to unwrap sandwiches and pickles, Jenny sucked in her breath and stopped what she was doing. She had the most powerful feeling of déjà vu. No, more an intense remembrance of a time in spring, on a day like this one, when she had been so hopeful, so full of anticipation. How different everything was now. She could never have imagined that day that she'd really be seeing Mr. Wonderful. That it really was possible to find love in such a short time. *And how quickly it could slip from my grasp. Oh, Andrew…*

Jenny realized that Karen was looking at her with concern again. Had she asked her a question?

"I'm sorry, I missed that. What did you say?" Jenny quieted her breathing and schooled her features to hide her emotion. This was supposed to be a pleasant day.

"I said, what's wrong? One minute we're giggling and planning dinner, the next you look as though you've seen a ghost. You alright?"

"I'm fine, really, just… I was remembering something. I was thinking back on that day in spring when I told you I was ready. Ready for Robert, it turns out." She tried for a smile, a wobbly and tearful smile. *Not Robert*. She couldn't lie to herself or to Karen anymore. Suddenly the confusion and pain and hurt she'd been holding inside gushed out. She poured out to Karen – her best friend, with whom she shared *almost* everything – all the worry and anguish she'd been hiding inside for the past months.

"Not Robert. He's not who I was thinking of. I *want* to think of him, and I want his to be the face I conjure in daydreams, but it's Andrew. I always see Andrew." Jenny tried desperately to hold onto her composure in the park while she spilled her heart out to Karen. "I love him, and I hate it. He's everything I want in a partner, but it's all wrong! I'm old enough to be his mother, for crying out loud. But, oh, my Lord, he is perfect. He's *perfect*. We can talk and joke or just sit quietly. We have so much in common, big things and little things. I like who I am with him. He's gorgeous, that's no secret, and I could stare at him all day." Her voice lowered as she confessed, "He kissed me once. Oh, my gosh, Karen, it was the most…" Her voice dropped again, to a whisper. "I have second-guessed pushing him away every single day since then. I know it was the right thing to do, but just once, I would like to have done something reckless. Like sleep with Andrew. Karen, am I awful? I can't stop thinking of it, and --" She stopped short of telling Karen her fantasies. "But Robert. He's perfect, too. I'm supposed to love *him*. I feel like he was an answer to prayer. He's everything I thought I wanted. Really. I like him – could maybe even love him. And if it weren't for Andrew, I'd probably already be head over heels."

She stopped to catch her breath and as she thought of the argument after Andrew's torrid kiss, and that terrible kiss goodbye. Andrew's cold shoulder since her return from Chicago ripped at her, and her tears flowed again. She blew her nose and continued on. "Andrew won't talk to me. He didn't return my calls after I got home from Chicago, he returned my house key, and as far as I can tell, has disappeared from the face of the earth. I haven't seen him for so long, haven't even bumped into him in town. I wake up wanting to see him and talk with him, secretly hoping we'll cross paths somewhere along the way, and being disappointed at bedtime when another day has gone by without him. I tell myself I should be happy with Robert; I should be thrilled with such a wonderful man. But he's not Andrew, and he never will be."

Words deserted her as she fought for control over her emotions. Her mind flitted over memories of Andrew and Robert. The tears ebbed, and her ragged breath became normal. Slowly, as she regained her composure, she realized that the burden had lifted, if only a little. She still hadn't come up with a solution.

Karen let the silence stretch as she took in everything she'd just been told. She had reached out early on, and held Jenny's hand in her own. She squeezed it in reassurance as she thought. *So much makes sense now!* Although some things were still in question, she understood little things, like Jenny's constant yammering about Robert. Whether Jenny realized it or not, she was trying to convince *herself* that he was perfect. Not Karen, and not anyone else. If it took that much convincing, he was obviously *not* perfect. Not for Jenny, at any rate. And Andrew – what a mess she'd made there.

"Alright, my dear. What are we going to do? This mess needs sorting out once and for all. Robert might be near-perfect, but it's clear he's not for you. And apparently, your heart thinks the perfect guy could be Andrew. You need to give him a chance."

Jenny maintained her silence, but a thousand thoughts were running through her head. She needed to talk to Robert. He really was a lovely man, he just wasn't for her. As if that wouldn't be hard enough, she'd follow up that conversation by tracking Andrew down and baring her heart. He may not care anymore, but she needed to know. Ugh. How had her simple life gotten so complicated? Though now that she'd shared with Karen, the obvious seemed so obvious. All the complication seemed so simple. She should have shared with Karen from the beginning, and not held all this in for so long.

"I'm sorry I didn't share with you earlier. It's just that Andrew felt like some sort of forbidden fruit, even though you'd told me to ogle him – ogle, not fall in love with him! Perhaps if I had talked to you, things would be different. Now, well, who knows. But I know I need to talk to him. His coldness is killing me. I ache. I *ache*. My heart hurts, like it did when I lost David, like it would if I lost you." Jenny teared up yet again at the thought of losing her best girlfriend. She looked at Karen to find her tearing up as well. The two friends hugged and cried and laughed at themselves for making such a loud public display. They gathered their things and strolled back to the library to freshen up and get back to work.

Dinner at Jenny's was lovely. Danny commandeered the grill, with Robert's help, and Karen and Jenny handled all the indoor preparations. They ate under the pergola with the stars beginning to peek out above, and a melodious chorus of crickets and night insects in the background. The two couples laughed and carried on, thoroughly enjoying dinner and the company of friends.

Toward the end of the evening, Jenny took Robert aside and spoke quietly to him.

"Robert, I've been thinking about us. I..." Jenny trailed off, unsure what to say. It had been a week; surely he assumed she'd thought and chosen him.

"I see. You don't have to say anything more. I can see it in your eyes. Darling, I'll be fine. I'm disappointed, of course, but it was only a matter of time before you followed your heart and not your head. It's what I admire so much about you."

"Robert, you really are Mr. Wonderful, aren't you?"

"Mr. Wonderful, huh?" Robert looked bemused. Jenny smiled and bashfully told him about his nickname.

He brought her close for a hug and whispered into her hair. "I might never let you forget that. I quite enjoy the thought of being Mr. Wonderful. Perhaps you can find me a Mrs. Wonderful, too."

Karen looked on as Jenny and Robert continued their quiet conversation, trying desperately to hear, while Danny tried equally to distract her from the couple. "Karen, you cannot eavesdrop on this one. Give the man a little privacy while he's having his heart handed back to him."

"I don't know, he doesn't look too heartbroken to me."

"The less heartbroken they look, the more they are. He's hiding it, saving face. Get it, Girlie? Besides, it's Jenny we're talking about. Of course he's in love with her. Who wouldn't be? Except for me; I have more woman than I can handle, right here in my arms. Kiss me, Kari Baby." He smiled at his wife and wrapped his arms more tightly around her.

"Oh, Danny. Sometimes you are a real romantic, you know that?" Karen snuggled up to him on the bench and kissed him full on the mouth. She didn't let up until she heard Jenny loudly clearing her throat. She and Robert were standing arm in arm in front of them with amused expressions on their faces.

Karen straightened up and looked them in the eye. They both looked no worse for wear. Actually, they didn't look any different than they had an hour ago. Maybe breaking up wasn't so hard to do, after all.

"What? Can't a woman kiss her husband when she wants? What's the point of being married if I can't kiss him all the time?" She turned to Danny again, and bussed his cheek. He stood and brought her up with him.

"Yeah, she wants me. It's a curse, but I live with it." Danny winked and curled his arm tighter around his Karen, more to prevent her elbow in his ribs than anything else. "Jenny, much as we hate to go, it's getting late. The older we get, the earlier I need to get to bed. Rob, you want a ride home, or are you good?"

"I'll take a lift, thanks. Just give me another moment, alright?"

Robert picked up the last of their glasses and walked with Jenny into the kitchen once more.

"Jenny, dear, thank you for dinner. And if you need me, I'm still in town for a few weeks, and I have quite enjoyed your company." He smiled and kissed her temple. "I'll see you around, then." With that he was out the door and stepping into Danny's car.

Karen met her at the library door in the morning. Jenny held back her laughter – she was frankly surprised that Karen hadn't called her last night. Danny must have kept her occupied. She smiled, and kept her silence until they got to her office. Sometimes keeping Karen on tenterhooks was a great deal of fun; she looked as though she was going to burst with her unasked questions. Jenny turned and sat down, and leaned forward as if imparting the juiciest gossip.

"Robert and I are on the best of terms. It helps that we talked a while ago about things. He was sort of expecting it. He really *is* Mr. Wonderful, by the way. Do you want to know a secret? He said he knew from the day I met him that I was not 'entirely free' – his words, not mine – but that he hadn't cared. Mostly, he'd just wanted to get me into bed that first night! Can you believe it?" Jenny had pondered those words over and over. She had resisted anything more than kisses from Robert, although those were quite delightful, but now that she knew he'd wanted to sleep with her, she was glad she hadn't, but it definitely made her feel sexy and womanly to have him want her like that. To think she'd thought he was shy about women!

"What? Oh, my dear Lord. You know, you still could. He's so handsome! Don't you want to know what he's like?"

"Karen, what is *wrong* with you? I can't just sleep with him now!" Karen said the most outrageous things! "That's… well, anyway – I don't want to. So there. He was very sweet though. If you really want a challenge, you should find him a match. Now, all I have to do is find Andrew. You know, this is crazy, but I feel so light and happy and…and fearless! I'm going to tell him how I really feel, and if he wants me, then that's wonderful. If he doesn't want me, I'll be okay. There will be someone for me. I know it." Jenny had woken this morning feeling more alive than she had in weeks. Just unloading all her worries with Karen had made all the difference.

"Well, I'm just happy your sparkle is back." She sincerely hoped that Andrew was willing to forgive and move forward with Jenny.

Andrew had just finished up an afternoon of putting in fence posts for Mrs. Petersen. He should have rented an auger, but it felt so good to use the old-fashioned post hole digger. He'd be sore in the morning, but it was worth it for a decent night's sleep. He was just cleaning up when Jenny cornered him. *Dammit*. He walked his tools over to his tool shed and hung them up neatly and slowly, trying desperately to gather his thoughts. After a moment she followed him in.

"You have to talk to me sometime, you know. And you're going to talk to me." She sounded, she thought, like a stern parent. Not a good way to start this conversation. Andrew must have thought the same thing. His voice dripped with derision.

"Am I? And say what? I can't begin to think what might be of interest to me. I'm sure your garden is fine. I taught you well enough. I talk to Josh enough to know he's moving next month, and I'll see him before he leaves. Do you have a leaky faucet? I'll get you the name of a plumber." If she was here to tell him she was getting married…no. He wouldn't even think it. It made him feel violent again.

Jenny was slightly taken aback but stood her ground. She shook, but she had been used to dealing with belligerent boys and men, and this one was no different. She had done nothing wrong, and he had no right to treat her like some sort of vermin, just because he was upset. Maybe he didn't deserve her love after all. She rethought her idea of telling him how she felt, but she certainly deserved an explanation from him regarding *his* behavior.

"You can start with telling me why you pretend I don't exist. And what I've done that you hate me."

At her words, all the fight went out of him. She thought he hated her. He could never hate her. He hated that she wasn't with him. He was definitely angry at her for not choosing him. He berated himself, *Andrew, yet again, you are an ass.*

"I don't hate you." His voice was pitched low. "Jenny, I can't be friends with you. But I don't hate you."

"Oh." *I can't be friends with you.* His words echoed in her head. So, he'd finally come to the conclusion she had always feared. He thought they were wrong for each other, just as she began to hope they'd be right. Her heart thudded loudly in her ears. She was too late. Jenny turned to walk away. It wasn't far to her house, and once she was safely locked inside, she could cry her eyes out. But not yet.

Andrew couldn't stand the heartbreak he saw in her eyes, but dammit, if she was going to be with Robert, he just couldn't go back to the way things were, and he couldn't see a way not to seethe with jealousy whenever he saw them together. "Jenny, wait. I am sorry for the way things ended. I am. But you know…You know I loved you." All the questions he'd had, the insecurities, the doubts and anger and hurt, somehow the big ones just came out. "Why? You barely knew him, and yet you thought he was a better man than me? I love you. I hoped you'd love me too. But you rejected me. And for *him*? All he wanted was to get under your skirt. Do you know that? I heard him talking one day. I wanted to kill him for having you. I saw him leave your house when you came home from Chicago. In the *morning*. Even I never stayed so late, no matter how much we talked. I thought," he lifted his gaze from the floor and stared intently into her eyes. "I thought, one day you'd really *see* me, that if I stuck it out long enough, if I was patient enough, you'd see how much I love you, how good we are together. But you don't see that at all. You don't see *me* at all. So, no. We can't be friends. I cannot be 'just another friend' to you because I will *always* want what Robert has. Jenny, I want you to be happy. More than anything, I wish *I* could have made you happy. Robert is a lucky bastard, and I hope he is everything you wanted."

Jenny listened with disbelief. It really *was* all about Robert. He was jealous, plain and simple. He thought she'd slept with Robert during that ill-fated trip to Chicago. *Son of a…* Now she was the angry one.

"You loved me? Then why didn't you *fight* for me? If you thought for one minute that he was not the man *I* thought he was, that he was looking to take advantage of me, you should have warned me. You should have *told* me! Friends tell each other the unpleasant truths, too.

And as far as getting under skirts, maybe you don't remember that night in my kitchen the same way I do. I'm pretty sure you wanted to screw me that night! At least Robert never got angry when I put him off. He never took advantage of me, I'll have you know, and he seemed at least to understand the concept of waiting until I was ready! I came here, *Andrew,* to tell you that I love you, I can't stop thinking of you, and I *miss* you. But you are not the man I thought you were. You don't understand me at all. I don't think I want a man who says he loves me but won't fight for me." She swiped at tears, refusing to let them fall in front of him. Her voice broke as she turned again to go, and Andrew almost missed her last words. "How could I be with him when I only thought of you?"

Andrew stood in the shed, cursing himself in the foulest language he could think of.

"Andrew Sommers?" Robert had been waiting for Andrew to finish installing the new server for Mark before approaching him. "I'm Robert. Campbell. From the finance department. Do you mind if we talk for a moment? It won't take long. I can walk with you."

"Sure. Jenny's friend, I know." Andrew couldn't think of a good reason to refuse, no matter that this man felt just a bit like his sworn enemy. He probably just wanted to talk shop, anyway.

Robert rubbed the back of his neck nervously, unsure how to begin. He was never unsure of anything, so this was new. He plunged ahead, hoping for the right words.

"You and Jenny, you're friends, too? Perhaps, very good friends." It was less a question than a statement.

Andrew nodded. He was distinctly uncomfortable with where this conversation might be headed. "Yes, well, she and I have been friends." Andrew replied. "We haven't seen much of each other lately."

"Yes, I know. And I'm sorry for that. I just wanted to say take good care of her. She's a special woman, and I hope you know how lucky you are that she cares for you." She'd been so kind, gentle with him and his heart, breaking things off the way she had. Jenny hadn't made excuses, or made up silly reasons. He could still hear her sweet voice. *I'm sorry, I adore you, and wanted so much to truly love you, but I've already given my heart. I didn't realize it was gone until it was too late. You deserve so much better than I can give. Can you forgive me?* He'd wanted immediately to give her some peace of mind, to be as gentle with her in return, to ease her guilt and perhaps help her cause. She'd helped him see that he wanted more. Perhaps not with her, but with someone.

"Thank you, but she's not mine to take care of." *Not after what I've said.* Andrew's chest burned in remembrance of his last conversation with Jenny. Why, oh why couldn't Robert have talked to him *before*?

"Yes, she is. Find a way to make things right, and she's yours." With that Robert nodded stiffly and turned to go. Andrew could only stand and stare after him for long minutes.

Chapter 19

Oh, how she missed him. Before, there'd been hope. Now there was an emptiness. How could she hope they'd be together when he didn't even know her? When he thought so little of her that he assumed she'd jump into bed with the first man to show interest? She should give him the benefit of the doubt. His generation was looser than hers had been, and even so, she was old-fashioned. But he hadn't given her any. He'd just assumed, and hadn't even asked. He probably *couldn't* have asked *that*, but he'd disappeared. Hadn't even tried to fight for her. Jenny's heart ached for broken hopes, and for a love that would never be.

She deserved a love that was stubborn and wouldn't give up, a lover who would fight for her and with her, if that's what was needed. How could he have known what Robert had intended and not told her? Did he think she wouldn't have listened? Maybe she wouldn't have, but Andrew hadn't bothered to try. He'd just given up on her. On them.

Even so, she missed how it used to be back when they were friends. She missed the teasing flirting man she'd gotten to know. The thoughtful friend who had caught her fancy. The mischievous boy who peeked through in playful moments, the quiet companion who understood when she couldn't explain. She missed her Andrew.

She was almost to David's spot. This time she'd come for quiet and solitude. Not to vent, or rage, or cry. Just to be with him in the peace of the day. She could always just *be* with him. She'd been able to do the same with Andrew, until…

Jenny pulled out the book she'd brought to read. She wasn't much for poetry, but it had seemed like the right book to pull from the shelf. It had been David's; he'd loved his poetry.

She spread her blanket and settled in, thinking she'd read some of his favorites. She didn't know what they'd be yet, but he'd always marked in his books – stars and notes to indicate favorites and translations, definitions or references. She'd know once she opened the old book. *A Collection of Love Poems.* Perfect.

Hmm, there were notes, but not so many stars as she'd hoped. *Here's one!*

Ah, David, silly silly man. Jenny read the title again, and smiled. "Jenny Kissed Me." She had forgotten all about this poem, though he'd recited it to her a few times. She only knew the last line, which had become an affectionate reference, and eventually she'd forgotten the rest.

Jenny kissed me when we met,
Jumping from the chair she sat in.
Time, you thief! who love to get
Sweets into your list, put that in.
Say I'm weary, say I'm sad;
Say that health and wealth have missed me;
Say I'm growing old, but add—
Jenny kissed me!
~ Leigh Hunt

In her mind's eye she saw flashes of them as a young couple, and remembered the playful arguments about who had kissed whom first. He had always insisted that she'd been the first to kiss him, that she was always impatient and that had been no different. She hadn't even waited for their first date to come to an end!

Perhaps it had been true. She had been head over heels in love with him by the time they'd managed to have a first date, so often had they talked on the phone. She knew that he had been The One, and she'd been sure of it from the start. Of course, young people are sure of everything – passionate, care-free and fearless. It's only with time, with living life, that one sees the uncertainty of things, and that life will throw you the occasional curve-ball. *If only I could be so sure this time…*

She flipped to the next starred poem, and wished she'd thought to bring a hankie. She hadn't expected to cry, except for the note on the side of the page.

I asked Jenny to marry me today. She said yes! I'm going to have this poem read at the wedding. My True-Love Jenny has my heart.

My true-love hath my heart, and I have his,
But just exchange one to the other given:
I hold his dear, and mine he cannot miss,
There never was a better bargain driven:
My true-love hath my heart, and I have his.

His heart in me keeps him and me in one;
My heart in him his thoughts and senses guides;
He loves my heart, for once it was his own;
I cherish his because it in me bides:
My true-love hath my heart, and I have his.
~ Sir Philip Sidney

Jenny quelled the tears, but then her nose ran. Where was a tissue when she needed it? *Drat! Where's a happy poem?*

Jenny flipped to another page to find something less emotional for her. *Ah! Sally in our Alley – that sounds just right.* That one was followed by others not marked that caught her eye. Between poems, she pondered and stared at the trees and birds and the squirrels that wandered ever closer as she sat. Enjoying the quiet, she felt at peace.

It's time to go home, I think. At some point during her time there, she'd realized that she needn't hold on to David so tightly. She'd let go in the spring, only to cling tighter when things hadn't been as easy this time as they'd been with him. When she'd been confused and hurt, she'd run to him as she always had. But it was time, past time, for her to love on her own, with no comparison to David, and without mentally deferring to him for approval. He wasn't here, and he couldn't care. She needed to make her own choice, for her own reasons, and for her own happiness.

She had long since gotten over the rush of anger at Andrew's confession and rant. She'd had time to see things from his perspective, and to re-think a few things she'd thought she knew. Her own insecurities regarding him had seemed so huge – though they weren't, in the grand scheme of things. Perhaps he had his own set of insecurities that had led him to let her go so easily. That is, if he'd truly loved her in the first place. As she thought back over the summer, she was sure he did. Perhaps it hadn't been in grand gestures, but in all the little things he'd done and said, knowing that they'd make a difference to her. *He loved me…I know he loved me.*

Jenny looked through the mail without much thought as she opened the kitchen door. A few bills, lots of junk today, and tucked in to all of it, a plain white envelope with a masculine hand. *Andrew? It couldn't be, but definitely not one of the boys.* She dumped everything on the table and opened it quickly, scanning for a name. There, a scribbled initial, A. She carried the letter into her room and sat at the edge of the bed. Why would he write? She stared at the pages with longing. She was afraid to read them, and yet compelled. That he'd taken the time and written so much marked its importance.

With a swift intake of breath, she unfolded the letter and began to read.

Dear Jenny,

There is so much I need to beg your forgiveness for that I am not sure where to begin. I guess I will start with the last few weeks. I have been a total ass. I let petty jealousy rule me, and I couldn't see past it. You had every right to see Robert. He was practically perfect in every way. Because of that, I was jealous that you liked him. I wanted you to see me, to love me, and to be with me, but I forgot that you cannot force yourself to love another person. It happens or it doesn't. I should have been a better friend. All I could see was that I was losing someone I care about, as well as losing the woman I love. I was not a good friend to you, and a poor excuse for a man in general. I am so sorry.

I have to apologize, too, for being angry with you that night in the kitchen. I would do so much differently that night if I could go back. And maybe, maybe things could have been different. You are right that I should have understood you better, especially your need to wait. Except that I didn't really hear it. All I heard was that you thought I was a kid, too young for you, and that you were embarrassed by my feelings for you. It took me a while to calm down and see things from your side.

I think I am most sorry for assuming things about you and Robert. I can only claim that the green-eyed monster was living in me. It poked at me and poisoned me and all I could think was that of course you'd want to be with him, he had everything, and he was just about perfect. He's another David Martin. I am not. Can you forgive me for being such a jerk to you? I don't deserve it, but maybe someday you can forgive me. I'm sorry. I can't say it enough.

Jenny, I need to tell you something. I want you to understand. I have loved you for as long as I can remember. Not just since the spring, but when I was in high school. Then, I guess it was a crush, but a sincere one, and I never forgot you. So when we started spending time together this year, and I really got to know you, can you imagine how I felt? The fantasy woman I loved was flesh and blood and still every bit as wonderful. I was in heaven. Except that I couldn't believe that you could really love me. Like me, yes, but I guess that's why I didn't fight for you. I didn't think you could possibly love me in the long run. Me, a skinny kid who's barely making ends meet, and who can't give you everything your heart desires. Not like Robert, who can afford to fly you up to Chicago, or hell, to Paris if he wants! I don't know much about culture. I can't take you to all the concerts and museums you enjoyed with him. (Karen kept filling me in against my will.)

I know a little poetry, and that's it. So, since I'm not that good with my own words, here's a poem for you. I don't know who it's by. The book said anonymous. I read it in a college English class, and always thought of you. I still think of you. I hope you don't think it's corny.

If you but knew
How all my days seem filled with dreams of you,
How sometimes in the silent night
Your eyes thrill through me with their
tender light,
How oft I hear your voice when others speak,
How you 'mid other forms I seek –
Oh, love more real than though such dreams
were true
If you but knew.

Could you but guess
How you alone make all my happiness,
How I am more willing for your sake
To stand alone, give all and nothing take,
Nor chafe to think you bound while I am free,
Quite free, 'til death, to love you silently,
Could you but guess.

Could you but learn
How when you doubt my truth I sadly yearn
To tell you all, to stand for one brief space
Unfettered, soul to soul, as face to face,
To crown you king, my king, 'til life shall end,
My lover, and likewise my truest friend,
Would you love me, dearest, as fondly in return,
Could you but learn?

Yours,
A.

Jenny smiled through tears. Her heart was full, if a bit sad. She had a lot to think about now. Lines from Andrew's poem echoed in her mind, and she thought it was interesting that today she had read more poetry than she'd read in the past ten years.

Perhaps it was the sign she'd been waiting for, just when she'd decided she was done looking for them.

Hadn't she just said so, not more than an hour ago? It seemed much more than a coincidence, though. So much more…

Chapter 20

Things were quiet at the library. Of course they were. It was a library, after all. But Karen was out sick, so even the fun they made up for themselves to pass the time was missing. It had been two weeks since Jenny had received the letter from Andrew. She'd seen him in the Reserve once while she and Karen were walking. They had exchanged a hello and that was all. She hoped that he had read love and forgiveness in her eyes as he passed, but she thought he probably hadn't. He'd passed so quickly, and they hadn't seen him again. She supposed he'd altered his schedule, too abashed to see her. Still, Jenny hoped. She wanted to talk to him, but was unsure how to go about it. He seemed to avoid her, but this time, she thought it was from shame, not jealousy. If only she could tell him that he had nothing to be ashamed of. Love made fools of everyone, young and old, and he was no different. She still cared for him, and wanted him to know. If much more time passed, and she was going to track him down again in his own back yard.

The library door opened, and Mrs. Petersen stood silhouetted in the sunlight. *Finally! A living soul!* Jenny rose to see how she could help today.

With a smile, she handed the woman her books and walked her to the door.

"And, Mrs. Petersen? If you see Andrew, could you tell him to stop by? I have, um… a leaky faucet that needs attention. I'd be ever so grateful." Mrs. Petersen turned in the open door. She put her tiny hand on Jenny's arm, and spoke. "My dear, I'm not blind. Just old. Andrew will come when he's ready. I'll tell him you want to see him, though. It might be exactly what he needs to hear." And with that she was off.

Jenny was dumbfounded. How in the world had Mrs. Petersen *known*? She was a canny old lady, that's for sure!

Her heart positively ached today. Ached. She longed to talk with Andrew, and yet, she couldn't bring herself to. Mrs. Petersen said he'd come when he was ready. She wished he was ready now. The longer he waited the more unsure she became. The certainty she'd felt a few weeks ago was weakened by a creeping doubt and fear. He couldn't possibly be a match for her, yet something about him touched her heart the way no one else had. Not even David, and she had loved him with everything she'd had within her. How could they have so much in common, be so perfectly matched, and have so many barriers between them? First and foremost was age. The age gap was something that she mostly forgot about, but it was there, and it would pop up occasionally like a big neon sign.

Another thing was his friendship with her son. Would that be an impediment? Jenny was sure it would be, at least at first. She was certain that Josh wouldn't take too kindly to his mother dating someone his age, especially someone who'd been a school friend. How would he react? He'd said he would accept whomever she chose, but he was going to be surprised. He was sure to expect someone her own age, someone like his father.

Someday she was going to remarry, whether it was Andrew or someone else entirely. The boys had to get used to the idea at some point. She and Andrew hadn't talked about marriage. Heck, they weren't even dating yet! She was already getting way ahead of herself.

Perhaps there weren't so many barriers, after all. Two, and they had more to do with how she thought others might react than to how *she* or *he* felt. Speaking of feelings, how *did* she feel? *Would* she marry him if he asked?

Jenny thought long and hard. Could she live every day with Andrew? He was certainly kind, thoughtful, and intelligent. He was funny, he made her laugh every day, and she was fully aware of the value of laughter in her life. He was quiet. They had spent evenings alone hardly speaking to one another in a comfortable silence. They had been wonderfully cozy evenings, and she cherished the memories. It was telling that they didn't feel the need to fill the quiet with conversation or cover over it with busy-ness. It was alright for them simply to be together.

She thought about the conversations they'd had about serious issues. He'd surprised Jenny by telling her he'd never really wanted children. She thought he'd make a terrific parent, and since that had been her heart's desire when she'd been young, it was a little hard at first for her to grasp that he didn't want the same thing. Andrew said he'd be content being a terrific uncle to his sisters' kids.

Finally, could she be intimate with him? She thought about him constantly. In her mind, they had been together a thousand times. She was afraid that, in reality, he might not find her nearly as attractive as she found him. While she took care of herself, and knew she was in decent shape, she wasn't twenty anymore and it showed. Could he, would he be alright with that, especially as they continued to age? She hated that she was being so shallow. It was much more important that he love her mind and heart, but that's the way it was. So be it.

If she couldn't talk to Andrew, she needed Karen. Karen would ease her mind and stop her from over-thinking every single thing that had been or not been done and said for the past few weeks.

"Karen thank you! Thank you for keeping me company today. I need to do some serious walking today. I'm turning into a basket case, waiting for him. I keep thinking of all the what-ifs and should-haves. I should just go to him. Shouldn't I?" The two were just finishing up their time in the Reserve. It was getting colder every day, and they didn't get out as much as they used to.

"Yes, yes you should. He must be waiting for you to make a move. He sent you that wonderfully romantic, perfectly apologetic letter didn't he? You need to respond, and I can't believe you haven't already."

"Yes, well, I had to deliberate first. Then we saw him, but he didn't stop, so I got nervous and had to deliberate all over again. Ugh! Why do I feel like I'm fifteen again? This is awful. Then there was Mrs. Petersen last week. I told you what she said. She said he'd come when he was ready. When *he* was ready! Why does it have to take so long?" Her impatience was showing. David was probably laughing at her from wherever he was.

Chapter 21

Andrew had spent the last three weeks, when he wasn't working himself to the bone, careening between complete horror at having sent Jenny such a pathetic excuse for a love letter and a somewhat hopeless hope that it had gotten lost in the mail. He was caught between the morbid certainty that she had read it and been completely unmoved, and anxious optimism that she'd come to him with open arms. With each day that passed, it seemed more and more likely that she wasn't going to come. He wanted to hope, but he was scared. He'd been such an ass. He'd seen her the one time at the Reserve, and had been so emotionally unprepared that he couldn't stop, his heart had leapt into his throat, and he could barely breathe. She must've thought, well, he had no idea what she thought, because he hadn't looked at her. He'd avoided the Reserve ever since. Uncertainty was the worst.

He spent his free time with the Petersens, something he hadn't done for much too long. Mr. Petersen was great – sometimes it was like stepping back in time, to when he was a teenager hanging out with Gramps. Mr. Petersen had the same way of telling stories and imparting wisdom. Especially wisdom about women. He had known without being told that Andrew was nursing a bruised heart. He would talk about his own journey to love with Mrs. Petersen. Apparently it had been a rocky start, not that you'd know looking at them now. They'd been married for sixty years, and were two halves of the same whole. It gave Andrew hope. Which, he supposed, was the whole point.

"Don't you worry, Boy. Sometimes it takes women time to come around. Give her space to know her mind, and love will be the better for it."

"How'd you know Mrs. P. was your soulmate?" Andrew and Mr. Petersen were sitting in the front room playing cards. Andrew was getting trounced, more like. He was terrible at Gin Rummy.

"Well, Boy, I'll tell ya the short and sweet of it. She makes me laugh every day. No matter that things have all gone to the crapper, she finds a way to make me smile. That's a rare thing, right there. And then, if that ain't enough, she lets me just be quiet. It's a good woman who understands that a man's only got so many words. Gin."

Andrew threw in his cards. "You win, sir. I can't take any more of this beating." He sat back and stretched his arms over his head and smiled at his old friend. Mr. Petersen smiled back.

Chapter 22

He was done waiting. Three weeks was plenty for her to know her mind and mull things over. It was time to talk. But before he went, he'd go see the Petersens. Just for a pep talk. He rapped on the back door and walked in. Mrs. Petersen was in the kitchen hovering over the stove. Something smelled delicious!

"Mrs. P. I'm so glad to see you. Just wanted to see if you need anything from the store while I'm out today.

Milk or bread? Bananas?" He kissed her uplifted cheek as he waited for her answer.

"No, nothing today. But you could take these books back to the library for me. I finished them already. Tell that nice librarian lady thanks for the books. Oh, and I forgot to tell you that she has a leaky faucet. You should probably check on it soon. Such a good boy." She patted his cheek and turned back to the stove.

Jenny? Or Karen? There were two nice librarian ladies, though only one that might ask about a faucet. Karen had already used that excuse twice. There was no way she'd use it again. It had to be Jenny. He wondered when she'd mentioned the faucet, if Mrs. Petersen was *returning* the books. *For Pete's sake, she probably thinks* I *don't want to see* her*! I've been sitting on my ass all this time and she's been waiting for me. Dammit…*

Mr. Petersen was much more helpful. "Go, Boy. Leaky faucet, my Aunt Hildy. She's a-waiting for you, sure. Look at you, a strapping young man, your heart in your eyes. What's not to love? I tell you what, Boy, if she tells you no, you bring her right to me, and I'll straighten her all out. Why, she can't do better'n a boy who loves her like you do.

"Thanks, Mr. P. I'll bring her right here anyway. I want you to meet her. Just don't try stealing her away with that fancy talk." He headed out the door and toward the library.

"Karen? Is Jenny around?" He called the library on his way over, just to make sure Jenny was there. He wanted to get the scoop, so as not to walk into a mine field.

"Andrew, where the hell have you been? She's been waiting for you to call her for ages! You two really need to get your heads screwed on straight and get together already. And no, she's not here. She left to go help Josh finish up the last of his packing. He's moving next week."

"No really, Karen, tell me what you honestly think." Sometimes it was harsh being on the receiving end of her bluntness. "I didn't know I was supposed to call. Mrs. Petersen forgot to tell me. Damn. I forgot about Josh. I'll have to give him a call, too. We're supposed to get together before he leaves."

"No worries. He's coming up for a going away thing once all his stuff is on the moving truck. It's also a kind of an engagement party for the two of them. If you make nice with Jenny, maybe you can come. But I mean *really* nice. You have a lot of making up to do, mister."

"Okay, I'll try catching her in the morning. If you talk to her, please tell her I called. Please. And don't forget." Andrew hung up, not caring if she caught the pleading note in his voice.

Andrew walked to the library and left the books in the book drop. He walked around town aimlessly at first, not sure what to do. He'd gotten himself all keyed up to talk to Jenny, and now he couldn't, not until tomorrow. He walked through the cemetery and found himself somehow standing in front of Mr. Martin's headstone. He didn't know why he had ended up here, but he couldn't just leave without paying his respects. So, in his head, he started a monologue. He didn't even feel foolish. It wasn't like he was speaking out loud. Once the words started, they overwhelmed him.

Do you remember the summer of my senior year? Josh and I were always in his room, or in the yard tossing a football. That was a hard summer for me, and I was really glad for his friendship, for the Martin family. You were the family I wish I had that summer. My parents are fine now, but they were really going through a rough patch then, and I wanted to be anywhere but with them. I don't think I ever said how tough it was, but I know she knew, and sometimes we'd just stand in the kitchen and talk. Talk about college plans, the upcoming football season, anything. And she listened. What I said was important to her in that moment. I think I might've fallen a little bit in love with your wife then.

She loved us. That's it. She loved us and we all – every one of Josh's friends – noticed it. She fed us, yelled for us to wash our hands before dinner and to clear the table, and to be careful with the croquet mallets! But she wasn't *our mother, and I'm not the only one who had a crush! When we talked, I felt, well, it was very good for my ego to have her pay attention to me, even if I was the only one with romantic feelings. I've been looking ever since for a girl who could measure up to her. There are plenty of women who are pretty, and smart and funny, but none of the ones I've found have as big a heart. Now I have a chance to make her mine. I hope you don't mind. I know you know how wonderful she is. She makes me smile. I love her. It's not the crush from my youth. I love her. I am so proud of how she has blossomed, even though I had nothing to do with it. She's so independent. You should see her. Still thoughtful, still sunny and optimistic. You should see it when she and Karen come home from a shopping trip. Jenny and her enthusiasm for dresses! I s'pose you'd know all about that, though. David, I love her. From the way she curses at pickle jars that are just slightly too big for her to open, to her choices in music, to the way she loves on her friends and family. She is so amazing. It sounds so corny, but it's true: I like who I am when I'm with her. She makes me want to be a better person. The person she sees, not the one I know I am. Will you give me a chance with her? David, I know it's crazy, but I'd feel better if I knew you were okay with us. I promise I'll love her better than anyone could. I will keep her safe, and hold her close to my heart for always. She is everything to me, and I am nothing without her.*

He wanted David to understand, to let her go, to give his blessing, if that was possible.

Andrew still wasn't entirely sure if Jenny wanted him, although Karen's words had been encouraging. He left Mr. Martin and walked home. As he passed Jenny's house, he noted that the kitchen light was on. She was home, but it was getting late. He'd stop by in the morning. He didn't think he could wait much longer.

Andrew saw the flashing lights as he turned the corner, and ran the rest of the way. He came up short at the back door of an ambulance, where EMTs were loading a gurney. Mr. Petersen lay there, oxygen mask in place and face grey. Mrs. Petersen was at his side holding his hand. She was being helped into the back by a young woman, whose task was made more difficult because the Petersens wouldn't let go their hands.

"May I?" Andrew reached in and picked Mrs. Petersen up without even a by-your-leave, and placed her up in the back. "I'll meet you at the hospital. I'll be there before you know it. Did you call the kids? Never mind. I'll call for you." He didn't know if they heard his words, but he left anyway. He was in his truck and on the phone before the squad car's doors had shut. He called their oldest son first, knowing Mike would be able to meet him at the hospital soonest, and let him take care of the others.

Andrew hadn't been to the ER, much less the hospital, since his Gram had gone in. He hated that he was back for too-familiar a reason. He didn't think Mr. Petersen would be going back home tonight, but hopefully he would pull through, and he'd be back at Gin Rummy in a week or two. He had to be. Andrew paced the waiting room, anxious for word. All the others had been allowed back, but he wasn't related, so…here he was. He was thinking about getting some coffee when he saw Mike slowly walking toward him.

Mike didn't look good. He looked, actually, like Andrew's dad had when Gramps had died. Like a man who'd just lost his father.

"They're going to move him. He's not good, not good at all, but they want to put him in a more comfortable room. Once they get him settled you can go in and see him. He's sleeping, but I know you've been like a grandson. He loves you, Andrew, and I know you love him."

Andrew sighed deep with relief. Mr. Petersen was hanging on. He'd make it through; it'd take more than a simple heart attack to do him in. Andrew refused to register that Mike didn't seem to hold out much hope.

The whole family spent the rest of the night in the little seating area outside of the ICU. They took turns looking in on him, as they could, one at a time. Visiting hours seem to have been extended for the Petersen clan. They'd situated their mother in the bed next to their ever weakening father, and it was enough to break one's heart to see them lying next to each other like that.

They kept vigil over him until late in the afternoon. Mr. Petersen – everyone was calling him Pops, and Andrew soon joined in for ease of conversation – awoke and rallied. He was asking for everyone to come in. He wanted to see his family, and sing a bit. But it wasn't long before he tired again and needed to rest. They rotated turns looking in on him once more. It was about 8:00 when Mike called to his siblings quietly. They filed in, just the four of them, and Andrew heard a low keening come from within. He knew. He'd heard exactly that sound the day Gramps had died. He felt so suddenly lonely and out of place. The Petersens all had each other, and though they'd allowed him to share in the vigil, he wasn't one of them. He stood and rubbed his eyes, clearing them as best he could, and left.

He drove straight to Jenny's. Andrew didn't think about it, just drove. There was only one place that was home anymore. The only place he wanted to be was with Jenny. He knew she'd understand; she was good like that. As he turned the engine off he thanked heaven that she was home. He could see her through the window as he reached the door. He gave a cursory knock and opened it himself.

Jenny turned from the stove to find Andrew standing just inside the door, looking anguished and beaten down. She rushed to his side and put her hands to either side of his face. "Andrew, Sweetheart, what is wrong? You look..." She was afraid to say how he looked. He looked as if someone had died, but who?

"I'm really sorry to barge in on you but...can we just..." He walked slowly to the living room and dropped onto the sofa, hanging his head in his hands. Jenny turned off the oven and followed him in, putting her arm about his shoulder as she sat.

"Tell me...something awful happened, I know."

"It's Mr. Petersen. He's...um..." His throat was closed up and he was on the edge of tears. The Petersens were his grandparents' friends – *his* friends. He'd known them all his life. And now, well, he didn't want to think of now. He didn't want to think at all.

"Oh, Sweetheart. I'm so sorry. I'm so, so sorry." She put her arms around him and held him close. "What can I do to help? What do you need?"

"Just…just sit with me. I'll be fine." They sat in silence for a long while, and gradually he began to talk. His worry over Mrs. Petersen, although she had her kids close by and was with them right now. Memories of Mr. Petersen, and of his grandfather. There was laughter, too, over Mr. Petersen's antics as he tried to pull a fast one on his wife, like sneaking a pipe when she'd made him quit, or a scotch after the doctor had said no more. More laughter, then a lapse into silence. "I am going to miss him. He was like my Gramps. And now he's gone." Tears threatened, but he wouldn't let them fall. It was getting late, and he should go, but Andrew couldn't seem to move. It was as though once he stepped outside, the grief would overwhelm him. He wasn't ready to deal with it tonight. As though she read his thoughts, Jenny spoke.

"Stay here. I know how hard it is to be alone with fresh grief. I'll get the guest room ready and order a pizza. Then we'll just sit and watch TV or a movie. Anything you want. I know all you really want is to forget for a bit." She phoned the pizza shop as she rummaged for fresh sheets and pillows for the guest room, made the bed while he sat with his thoughts and put a clean towel in the bathroom. It would be like having one of the boys home for the weekend. *Only he's not one of the boys.* She shut that thought away in the recesses of her mind. For tonight, he only needed to be taken care of, so she would take care of him.

They watched old reruns and ate pizza until it was past time for bed. She needed to be up for work in the morning.

"Come on, Sweetheart. It's late. There's a new toothbrush laid out for you, and a towel, anything you might need is in there." Jenny pulled at his arm to lift him from the couch.

"No, I'm not ready yet. You go on. I can find my way. And Jenny…thank you." He squeezed his eyes shut for just a moment to clear the emotion welling once again. "Thank you."

"Hey, what are friends for? If you're sure?" He smiled his assurance that he was fine, and she padded off down the hall. She could hear the TV once again, some sci-fi slasher movie he'd found by the sound of it.

Jenny woke to the sound of a scream and sat bolt upright. *Oh yes, the television.* She felt for her wrap and pulled it on as she made her way back to the living room. Andrew was still on the sofa, bare feet up and eyes closed, hand loosely around the remote, dozing. She leaned over and touched his knee. "Hey." She called softly at first, almost a whisper. "Andrew, Sweetie, it's midnight. Bedtime. Come on." She turned off the television and sat next to him. A little louder, "Andrew…" Slowly his eyes opened. She teased him, "You should be in bed if you're so tired."

"I can't. Here is fine. The TV is keeping me company, and the noise keeps me from thinking. Just turn it back on. I'll watch info-mercials if that's better for you." He reached for the remote in her hand.

"Oh, Sweetheart. You can do whatever you want. You sure you wouldn't rather sack out in bed? No? All right. I'll see you in the morning, then." She reached over and hugged him. He gave a shuddering breath, the sort that usually meant tears, but he didn't cry, just held on for a long moment. As the moment stretched, she squeezed him and made to let go, but he held on tight.

"Don't go, not yet. Please."

"Okay." Jenny thought back to a night long ago when her favorite aunt had died. That night, David had tucked her into bed, then laid down beside her and held her all night. More than held her, actually, and she remembered the bliss of forgetting the heart's pain in the body's pleasure.

Jenny tried to stifle the thought. She knew what was right and proper, too, and that was not it. But once she'd thought it, her body, starved for so long of the solace of intimacy, began to heat. She knew he would not say no.

He would welcome it. He might regret it later, but for now he needed her, not as a mother or even a friend, but as a lover. Jenny acted before she thought any more. Turning her face into the crook of his neck, she kissed him the way she'd once dreamed of doing. Opening her lips the slightest bit, tasting his skin…

"God, Jenny, please! You have no idea…" His voice was ragged. The moment he realized her lips were on him, he hardened. If this was a dream, he never wanted to wake up. She didn't stop, only nuzzled further. She slid her mouth over his neck, nipping and tasting her way up to his jaw. He raised his hands to her face and brought her lips to his, devouring her in his need. She matched him perfectly, knowing just when to give and when to take, exploring his body with roving hands until their kisses slowed. The immediate heat and fire of sudden desire was banked for the moment, but was by no means extinguished. "Jenny…"

"Hush…I know. No thinking tonight. Whatever happens, happens. Only let me take care of you. Let me help you forget, just for tonight." She spoke in soft tones, soothing and seductive. How could he possibly say no? In answer, he kissed her again, slowly threading his fingers through her hair. She let him explore, with kisses and caresses falling over her face, down her neck and onto her shoulders and collarbone. She reveled in the feel of his touch, taking pleasure in every moment, allowing herself to be fully with him, with no thought other than to give and receive pleasure with Andrew.

Jenny pulled gradually from his touch. She had meant to tend to his needs. She clasped his hand and brought it to her mouth, kissing the palm and the inside of his wrist. She whispered softly to him, "Tell me what you want. I want what you want." She brought his index finger to her lips and sucked delicately on the tip. "Do you like this? Tell me..."

Andrew was mesmerized by the sight of her mouth as she pulled another finger between her lips. He felt her tongue swirl around it and he closed his eyes. He wasn't sure he was actually capable of speech at the moment, but he tried. *Yes, yes! I love it!* Instead of the words, he heard a low groan come from his throat. She continued her exploration of his hands, removing the one from her grip and placing it on her upper thigh as she began the process again on the other. *Incredibly seductive...*this was the only way to describe what she was doing. He would not have thought this simple thing would leave him wanting so much more. But her mouth...he wanted that mouth on him everywhere. His skin burned at the thought and he grew harder still.

His free hand tightened on her thigh and began a slow exploration of its own, across her hip and down over her buttock, then back up and across her waist to her ribs. His fingers stopped just shy of their target, the vee of his index finger and thumb resting on the underside of its curve. With his fingertips he caressed the side of her breast, moving incrementally inward, torturously slow, whisper-soft. Jenny moaned her own desire, and nipped at the pad of flesh at the base of his thumb. "Touch me. Please." She flattened his hand and pressed it to her chest.

Too many clothes. Jenny was intent now on undressing Andrew, seeing him and touching him and tasting him. She released his hands to unbutton his shirt. Finally she managed to pull it free from his trousers and push it back over his shoulders. She'd seen him work shirtless on countless occasions, and had often wondered what the wiry muscles would feel like under her hands. They felt hot and hard and supremely masculine. He was absolutely beautiful, there was no other word for him. Almost of their own volition, her hands smoothed over his shoulders, his chest, to his belly. She saw the bulge in his pants and wanted desperately to touch. She skimmed the tips of her fingers over the fabric covering him before returning her attention to his chest. The flames were licking at her again, and she was losing patience. *This is for him, not you,* she reminded herself, willing herself to slow the tempo, to pay attention to his needs and wants, to give him pleasure.

"Tell me what you want, my love." She stroked his skin, taking note of the gooseflesh that had risen, the way the small male nipples hardened under her thumbs.

"You. I want you." He grabbed her waist and pulled her over him. He wanted to feel her body against his, hip to hip, breast to chest, lip to lip.

Jenny twined her arms around him, straddling his thighs and fitting her hips close to his. She kissed him, hard and hot, pressing herself onto the ridge of his erection, rocking against him, escalating desire for both of them. Andrew met her, matched her. What he wanted was to strip her naked and slide into her this instant. Her nightshirt had ridden up, barely covering her legs. Skimming his fingers under the hem and grabbing her derriere, pushing his hips into hers, he growled need into her mouth. "Now, I want you now." Andrew released her long enough to unfasten his trousers. Fumbling between them, he pushed them down his hips to free himself.

Sliding his hands up the insides of her thighs, he used a thumb to pull aside the thin fabric of her panties. He wanted inside her, right now, this instant; he had wanted it five minutes ago. Knowing his need, she fit him to her opening and sheathed him in her warmth. After so long, she thought it would be more difficult, but she was wet and ready and on fire for him. Andrew's hands were on her waist, moving her up and down at a quickening pace, her moans and gasps fueling his ardor and feeding the climax building inside him. He couldn't hold back any longer. He drove upward with his hips, once, twice, three times, holding her as tightly to him as he could, pumping into her and crying out his release. At last his hips relaxed back onto the sofa and he loosened his tight grip. His hands circled around her back and pulled her into his chest. He kissed her and stroked her back, tangled his fingers in her hair, stunned at what had just taken place.

"Sweetheart are you alright?" he murmured. "I didn't mean to be quite so intense, but, you are just so hot. I promise to take better care next time." Andrew spoke lazily into her hair. It was rather presumptuous of him to assume there would be a next time, but there had to be. He wanted – no, he needed – more of her.

"Mmm…yes. I feel wonderful." She answered with a smile and equal lassitude. She needed more, wanted her own climax, too, but the feeling of fullness and the warm afterglow of sex had sated her for the moment. She kissed him and let her hands wander across his shoulders. She pulled away and looked coquettishly into his eyes. "Bed. We need a bed for next time. The sofa won't be nearly big enough for what I have in mind for you, my love." She reluctantly lifted herself from him and stood on wobbly legs. Taking him by the hands she pulled him from the couch. "Hmmm, I think…" She tucked him back into his pants and redid the top button, dressed just enough to move them both the few feet it took get to her room, then took his hand again and led him to her bed, turning him to face her. She undid his trousers once more, shucked them off his limbs in one quick motion, and pushed him back onto the mattress so that she could pull them completely off.

"I'll be right back. Don't go anywhere." Jenny scampered across the hall to the bathroom. She grabbed a hand towel and swiped at the stickiness on her thighs. She caught sight of herself in the mirror. Her nightshirt was positively frumpy. She'd worn it on purpose. But now, she closed her eyes and quick as lightning removed her wrap and shirt. She was naked except for her thin lace panties. She looked again. *Nope, those go too.* With a deep breath she squared her shoulders and scampered back into her room. In a flash, she was in bed and under the sheet, skin to skin with an also-very-naked Andrew. He was lounging in the center of the bed with his hands behind his head, and she was now pressed up against his side. She'd bent a leg over his hip and wrapped an arm across his chest without thought.

"Oh my God, you're not wearing anything, are you?" Andrew had taken stock of things while she was gone. It had been a mere minute, but that had been long enough to realize that he'd just made love to, and was now *in bed with,* the most amazing woman on earth.

Jenny was extraordinary, and she'd given herself to him at long last. She may not know it yet, but she was his, and he would never let her go.

"Um, no. Not a thing." Jenny's heart was racing, whether from fear or anticipation, she didn't really know. Maybe both.

Andrew was on her in less than a heartbeat, covering her warm, luscious body with his. He was stiffening all over again and pressing into her. His mouth was on hers, demanding and plundering. He wanted to touch her everywhere, to ravish her. She made him wild with want. He felt like a rutting animal, yet, he couldn't hold back. Jenny, too, felt wild and wanton and almost violent. She didn't remember ever feeling so greedy before. She spread her legs for him, cradled him between her thighs and wrapped herself around him, as eager as he was. She lifted her hips, pushing against him, and moaned into his mouth, begging for him to enter her. They made love once more, frantically and desperately, before collapsing into each other's arms.

In the early hours before dawn, Jenny slipped from the bed and into the kitchen. The day would intrude before long, but she was intent on keeping it at bay for as long as she could. She texted Karen:

> *Not coming in today. No questions, no calls.*
> *Talk to you later. Love you. <3*

Jenny slid back into his arms and once more fell into a deep sleep.

Andrew woke her in the morning with a whisper and a stroke of hand over hip. "Sweet Jenny, my love, are you awake?" He dusted kisses over her face, teased her ears with nibbles and murmurs of love, tangled his fingers in her long dark hair. "Jenny…my Jenny…"

Jenny was awake, had been awake, but was loathe to open her eyes. His sweet attentions made her heart ache in a wonderful way. She loved this man, more than she'd thought possible, and she was afraid. Afraid to love so much, and afraid not to. She should have known that what she'd begun last night would have such an impact. She was never one to give over her heart lightly. David had been her first serious boyfriend, and then her husband, and her true friends could be counted on one hand. She should have known that what she'd meant as one night of caring would bind her irrevocably to him. Or perhaps she had known and welcomed it, in her heart of hearts. His teasing voice intruded on her thoughts again.

"I know you're awake. Kiss me good morning. Kiss me, or I'll find all the secret ticklish places you're hiding. Perhaps here?" He nuzzled her at the juncture of neck and shoulder. She held her breath to keep the giggles at bay. "Or here…" His searching fingers teased the sensitive hollows beneath her arms, and lower, squeezed at her waist. Her body shook in silent mirth. He shifted his focus to the joining of her hip and thigh.

"No!" Her eyes shot open and she sat upright, her face alight with suppressed laughter. "Please, no more tickling! I'm awake!" She giggled and turned him onto his back to return fire, finding his ticklish spots with startling accuracy.

"Jenny! Mercy! You win!" He wrapped his arms around her to prevent her further assault, and pulled her atop his chest to kiss her soundly on the lips. He pushed her heavy hair from her face and cradled her head in his hands. "You win." With smiling eyes and mouth he studied her face. "God, you are beautiful! How do you manage to be so gorgeous first thing in the morning? And after a sleepless night?" He growled suggestively and rolled them over, covering her again in kisses, bent again on seduction instead of play.

Chapter 23

Jenny and Andrew sat across from each other at the kitchen table having breakfast. It was late, almost mid-morning, but today time was meaningless. They were together, and that was all that mattered. Jenny couldn't stop smiling, feeling much like the cat that ate the canary. Andrew had insisted on fixing her breakfast this morning, cheese omelettes with toast. She thought it was the most delicious breakfast she'd had in a very, very long time.

Andrew was toying with the twist-tie from the bread bag. He was in a pondering state, even if he couldn't wipe the smile off his face. His first thought this morning was that if this was his last day on earth, he'd die a happy man. His second was that he wanted to wake up next to Jenny every day for the rest of his life. To that end, he had a question to ask the woman across from him. But how and where to ask? *Screw it – I gotta ask now or I'll explode.*

"Jenny, my love..." Andrew slid from his chair to kneel at her side. He held out the ring he'd fashioned from the twist-tie. "Will you marry me?"

Jenny reached slowly for his hands. "Andrew... Oh, Sweetheart..."

She couldn't say yes, could she? She wanted to say yes, with all her heart. She knelt next to him, drew him in and let him circle her with his arms as she fit the makeshift ring onto her finger. Holding it out to admire it as though it were the shiniest jewel she'd ever seen, she flashed a playful grin and answered. "Well, I don't know. Will I still have to pay you to work in my garden?"

"You can pay me in kisses." He bent his head to her neck and grazed smiling lips along her skin.

Jenny's eyes closed and the playfulness dropped for a moment as desire washed over her. Was there anything more seductive? If he did that every day, she'd be a fool to say no.

Jenny wrapped her arms tightly around his neck and returned his kiss, then spoke gently and warmly, but seriously.

"I want to say yes. I love you, but we have an awful lot to talk about first. Things most couples talk about *before* the engagement. Can we talk about those things before I give you an official yes? I do love you, Sweetheart."

Andrew released the breath he'd not realized he held. *She said yes!*

"We can do anything you want, take as long as you want, so long as I eventually get an official yes. I love you, Jenny." Andrew squeezed her tight, and all the emotions he'd held at bay for the past couple days, the intense joy of being with Jenny, the profound grief at his friend's passing, and every emotion between, bubbled up to the surface and overflowed. Tears he'd tamped down over and over again rose up and he was helpless to stop them. He cried, and she cried, and they both laughed, and through it, they held each other there on the kitchen floor.

Eventually they'd had to shower and dress. The rest of the world hadn't stopped for them, and there were quite a few things that needed to be taken care of before they could return to each other. There was Mrs. Petersen to check in with, and parents to call with the sad news. He'd gotten a call from Mark about a computer problem that needed fixing, and a lady whose bathroom doorknob had come off in her hand. Jenny still had a small party coming to her house Saturday, and she needed to go to the library, if only to tell Karen about her new fiancé. *Fiancé. It sounds so strange.*

Remarkable, to think how much had changed in a day, a week, in a year. Changed, yes, and now she was excited, even if a little nervous. She laughed out loud. If this wasn't fearlessness, she didn't know what was. But she also felt content. There was a deep sense of peace in her soul when she thought of a lifetime ahead with Andrew.

"Karen, I–" Karen interrupted Jenny with an enormous hug.

"I am so happy for you, Jen! Look at you! You're practically glowing! I am so glad you two finally talked to each other. You did talk, didn't you? At least a little bit?" There was a naughty gleam in her eye at the last question.

"How in the world? I haven't even told you anything yet!"

"You don't have to! I got your text, so naturally I drove by your house and saw his pick-up in the back. You vixen, you! I don't want the details, but tell me all about it! Oh, he's so young and virile. I bet it was *scrumptious*!"

"Oh my gosh, Karen! You really *are* incorrigible!" Jenny was both abashed and pleased that Karen knew already, although she only knew in part. There was time enough later for the whole story. For now, she contented herself with telling Karen just that they'd come to an agreement. She held to herself the secret pleasure of knowing she'd be his wife. Karen agreed to come over the next night to help her ready the place for the party, with the promise that she'd get the full scoop then.

"I'll see you in the morning." Jenny said. "Bring Danny tomorrow night, and the four of us will have dinner. He can sit and supervise if he doesn't want to work." With a smile and a wave, she was off.

Andrew greeted Jenny with a kiss at her kitchen door. "I missed you," he told her. It had only been a few hours, but she'd been all he could think about. Even when he'd been with Mrs. Petersen, in his mind's eye he pictured the laughing face of his Jenny. He wished Mr. Petersen could have met her. It was one thing he regretted. He'd dragged his feet, and now, well, Mr. Petersen could look down from heaven and see her. He knew his friend would approve. She was a perfect fit for him.

His mind was brought back to the very busy present by Jenny's questions. "When is the funeral? Do you want me to go with you?"

"Saturday morning. Of course I want you to come with me. It's a busy day, though. Are you sure you'll have time?"

"Yes. Karen and Danny are coming over tomorrow to help get the house ready. Well, Karen is helping. Danny is just coming over for food. You can keep him company if you like. Then I will have all Friday night to finish whatever else needs to be done. I just wish the weather was warmer. It would be so nice to have the party outdoors. Not so much to rearrange then. At least it's small, I think. I don't really know who Josh invited! I guess I'd better call and ask.

Andrew, I always have time for you. This is important. Are your parents going to make it up?" If there was one thing that worried her more than her boys' reaction, it was what Andrew's parents would think of their son with a much older woman. She had no idea what they would say. She had a feeling they might not like it so much. Honestly, she would think twice about it, too, if she were in their shoes.

"They'll be up Friday. Sweetheart, don't worry. I can see those wheels turning and you're worried what people will think. It doesn't matter what they think. When they see how good we are together, they'll come around. Alright?" He, to be honest, was also worried what people would think. Josh and Ryan were his chief concerns. His own family, he could handle. But those two? Eventually they'd get used to the idea. He gave Jenny a reassuring squeeze.

That night as they lay in bed, Andrew cradled her in the crook of his arm while Jenny played with his hands. She loved his hands, and remembered vividly the morning in the Reserve when he'd held hers while they sat in silence and pondered. She'd thought then that they were a perfect fit. She brought a hand up to her lips and kissed it.

A thought occurred to her. "Sweetheart, where will we live?" *I like my house. I don't want to move.*

She knew it was selfish. She would move if he wanted. But she rather hoped he didn't.

"Wherever you are is home to me. *You* are my home, Jenny Love. Where do you want to live? Here? Or shall we pick up stakes and move to California? I would live on the moon if you wanted us to." He kissed the top of her head. It was the truth. He thought of this as home because she was here. The place where he lived was still his grandparents' house to his mind. It had never felt like his own place. Their furniture was still in it, and he'd hardly changed a thing.

"Here. I want to live here," she replied. "This will be our home. Can I tell you something I only recently realized? When I bought the house, and the owners told me about you, I thought, *Well, how about that? The house comes with its own gardener and handyman*. So silly, but, to me, you have been here the whole time. You have helped me feel at peace here from the very beginning. I just didn't recognize it for what it was until I really *saw* you. You can thank Karen for that!"

"Oh, really? And what, exactly, should I thank her for?"

Jenny turned into him and let her hands wander. "She pointed out what a great pair of legs you have." Her hands stroked down his thighs. "And she commented on what a nice butt you have." Her hands stroked up to his hips and splayed out to caress his fabulous glute muscles. Pushing him onto his back, she straddled his hips, moving her hands to his chest. "And she told me to ogle you. And after I ogled you," she waggled her eyebrows suggestively, "I wanted to feel all those hard, lean muscles for myself. And I wanted you to kiss me. And other things…" She demonstrated all the other things she'd wanted to do with him…

Jenny couldn't sleep. There was so much yet to work out. She shouldn't be sleeping with him. The first night had been different. That was a night separate from all others and a special circumstance. Tonight it had seemed so natural that he should stay. They'd fallen so easily into it, their old routine for dinner, followed by their usual companionship. Instead of walking him to the door, though, she'd locked it and led him into her room again. There was an element of newness, yet it seemed as if they'd been doing this always, at least for her. She'd been married before. She was not unused to the habit of sharing the night hours with her lover and husband, yet she worried that she was rushing him in her eagerness to have that again. She enjoyed the weight of him next to her, feeling the warmth of his body wrapped around her.

She had gotten used to sleeping alone, it was true, but she had never really liked it. Now Andrew seemed all too willing (of course he was, he was a hot-blooded man, and she was a more-than-willing woman) and making love with him was incredible, but it wasn't right. Not until they made everything official. She wanted to say, not until they were married. But he was so attentive that if they weren't married very soon she didn't think she'd be able to hold out much longer.

She felt an arm snake over her hip and pull her in close, weakening her resolve with seductive tenderness. *Tomorrow.* She would talk to him tomorrow; he'd understand. It didn't hurt that they couldn't be together this weekend anyway. She'd have her boys here and Andrew's parents would be staying with him. Thank God for family.

After dinner, instead of "supervising," a grumbling Danny was pressed into service with Andrew to move furniture. Jenny and Karen thought rearranging the living room would help with traffic-flow for the gathering. When the ladies were satisfied with the lay-out, they all sat down to dessert.

"Whatcha got there on your finger, Jen? It looks suspiciously like a bread-bag thingy." Danny had a very good idea what it was, but he just wanted to hear her say it out loud. He was feeling ornery tonight. It was obvious that something was going on with his two friends. They couldn't keep their eyes off each other, though they were doing a creditable job with their hands.

Jenny twisted the bit of wire and plastic on her finger. She had worn it ever since Andrew had put it there and had gotten used to feeling it against her skin. It's not that she'd forgotten it was there, but she had rather forgotten that it wasn't a real ring, or that others could see it.

With a glance at Andrew, and a chagrinned look at Karen, Jenny took a breath and said "Andrew and I are engaged. It isn't official until we get some details worked out, so I didn't want to say anything, but..." She looked again at Andrew – she was grinning ear to ear, and so was he.

"Jennifer Ann Martin! I cannot believe you didn't tell me *immediately*! And here I thought we were best friends." Karen swooped on Jenny and hugged her tight, then flew over to a surprised Andrew to give him the same hug. "What needs to be worked out? Oh...you haven't told the families yet, have you? Oh, boy." Karen thought about what Josh and Ryan would have to say. She thought it might involve harsh words and curses. Directed at Andrew, not their beloved mama. They'd get used to it, especially when they saw how much love there was between these two.

"I want to wait until after the party; that should be about Josh and Emily. Oh, I can't believe Josh is moving, and getting married. Times they are a'changin' as the old song goes."

"I guess I had better take the ring back then, until after the party. If we don't want to make an announcement yet." Andrew had his hand outstretched, and Jenny reluctantly removed her ring. She moved to place it in his palm, but at the last moment pulled back.

"No, no, I'll keep it safe, if that's alright. I'll stash it in my jewelry box. Do you mind?" It was a silly thing, but she didn't really want to give it up. She was afraid he might throw it away. It wasn't a precious two-carat diamond, but it was special to her. He'd proposed, an honest to goodness, heartfelt proposal, with this scrap of wire. Jenny excused herself to put it away.

It was soon time for them to leave, and Andrew was the first to go, afraid if he waited until Karen and Danny left, it would be too easy for him to stay. He wanted to stay, and knew Jenny wanted it, too. Just, not quite yet. She was right. They needed to slow down. It was too easy to play house and sweep the small issues under the rug, or lose sight of practical things in the haze of desire. Oh, but that haze. He wouldn't get much sleep tonight. His mind would be reliving the last two nights of pleasure. He wondered how soon he could get her to the altar.

Jenny was finishing up the last of what prep she could do. She had washed every piece of silverware in the house and put them in a basket on the buffet, she'd rinsed and dried every punch glass and tumbler she had, and had the punch made and refrigerated. Veggies and fruits were chopped and artfully piled on platters, and bowls of nuts and chocolates were out and covered. Andrew had swept and cleaned up the patio, just in case people wanted to step out. It would be chilly, but not too cold. Things were as ready as they could be for tomorrow. She had a short list of things to be done in the afternoon, but she could have her usual breakfast with Karen before she got ready for the funeral.

She took one last look around the kitchen before joining Andrew on the sofa for a much needed rest.

"Thank you for helping! It's so much easier with two." She laid her head on his shoulder and closed her eyes. This, she could get used to. Relaxing after a day of work. She'd enjoyed a measure of it with their quiet evenings through the summer. Soon enough it would become an everyday routine, one she hoped not to take for granted.

"Anything for you." He smiled and laced his fingers with hers. "I'd better get going though. My parents will be home from dinner with my sister soon and will wonder where I am. I only told them I was coming to help you. I haven't told them about us. I will, though. Promise."

He stood, drew her up and led her into the kitchen.

"Come here. One last kiss to remember me by." He closed his arms around her and kissed her slowly.

Oh my… Jenny's heart thumped. This was no simple goodnight kiss. It was a torturous, devastating, seductive kiss, so much like their very first. He deepened it, pulling her as close to him as he could, one hand tangled in her hair and the other centered firmly below her waist, rocking his hips into her. He growled low and nipped at her lips as he pulled away. But Jenny wasn't done yet. She pulled him back in, wanting to devour him, too. She moaned, knowing that he loved to hear her desire, wanting so much more from him. She wanted him to press her up against the wall and have his way with her.

They didn't hear the door open behind them. Ryan stood there, momentarily stunned at the sight of his mother being mauled by a stranger. His mother! He roared as fury spurred him into action. He grabbed the bastard by the shoulders and whipped him around, pinned him up against the wall with one arm while he threw a mean right cross with the other. It was only as he pulled his fist back for another that the screams of his mother began to penetrate the haze of his fury. She was practically hanging on his arm, and yelling something in his ear. He dropped his fist, but kept the man against the wall. He asked if she was alright. Who knows what would have happened if he hadn't walked in. Ryan could see that though the man was small, his mom was no match for the intruder's wiry strength.

"Dammit, Ryan, what are you doing? Stop it! I said don't hit him!"

"MOM! He could have raped you. You're lucky I got here when I did!" He turned back to the man pinned up to the wall, and gave him a good pound against it. "You…I know you. Sommers! What the hell are you doing to my mom, you bastard!" He pounded him again. Jenny's hands bit into Ryan's arm and she tugged as hard as she could, to no avail.

"Ryan, let go of him! I'm telling you, he is with me, and he was just leaving. Let. GO!" She yanked again, and this time, he finally loosened his grip. Andrew folded and put his hands on his thighs, struggling to catch his breath. Jenny was at his side, fussing over him and poking at his cheek. *Oh…that is going to look awful in the morning!*

Jenny turned and laid into Ryan as only a mother could. She backed him up and into a chair so that she could yell at him from the advantage of height, something she hadn't had on him since he was twelve. Ryan was thoroughly confused, and feeling rather guilty, though he wasn't sure why. He had been so tickled at the thought of surprising her tonight instead of coming down tomorrow as planned. Then he thought he'd done a good thing, protecting his mom from danger, but it turned out he'd jumped to a wrong conclusion. Very wrong. She hadn't been in danger, and further…*she* was kissing *him*? *Sweet Jesus. This is not the surprise I thought it was going to be…* Ryan thought he was going to be sick.

"You're sleeping on the couch tonight. I have the guest room all made up for Emily tomorrow, and I don't have time to change the sheets in the morning. Go find yourself a blanket while I get Andrew taken care of. And don't talk to me right now. I might bite your head off again."

Jenny turned her attention back to Andrew, and immediately her face and voice softened. She walked him to a chair, though in Ryan's opinion the guy could damn well walk himself to a chair. It was just a bruise. Ryan didn't like feeling confused, and he didn't like all the fussing either. Unless it was over him. He stalked out of the kitchen to the linen closet and yanked a blanket and pillow off the shelf. The picture of his own mom with *that guy* was stuck in his head. Now that he'd been apprised of the situation…*ugh.* The Sommers kid was – what the hell was he doing with Mom? *What the hell?* Ryan didn't know what to think.

Andrew was trying to get Jenny not to fuss. "It's not so bad. I'm sure it looks worse than it feels." *And it feels like I got hit with a sledgehammer. Damn those Viking ancestors!*

"Sweetheart, you need to ice it down. I'm sorry I don't have a steak you can put on it; an ice pack will have to do. What is your mother going to say? Oh dear Lord.

And I think I'm going to have to explain you to my boys sooner than I thought. Why can't this be easy?"

"Hey, it's fine. I have been anticipating that punch for years now. When I think back to high school and all the fantasies I used to have about you, I was terrified that Josh would find out and clobber me. Of course, Josh is smaller and gentler than Ryan, but nonetheless, he's got a killer jab. Can we tell Josh when I'm *not* two feet in front of him? Maybe over the phone?"

"Aww, Sweetheart. Josh isn't going to hit you. He knows I'm seeing someone. I think he'll be far more understanding. Ryan didn't even know I was seeing anyone. He might just as easily have hit Robert. And you…wipe that smile off your face. Robert is nice. Not as nice as you." Jenny smiled her just-for-Andrew smile and kissed him gently near the swelling cheek. "I'm sorry my son hit you. It won't happen again. And, Sweetheart, there's not a chance your mom would react the same way? Should I wear a facemask tomorrow to meet her?"

Laughing, even when things were "in the crapper" just like Mr. Petersen had said.

"Have I told you today that I love you? Jenny, you are worth getting hit by a thousand Viking sledgehammers." Jenny looked confused, but laughed anyway, and Andrew kissed her one last time before walking himself home with an ice pack on his face and a smile on his lips.

Chapter 24

"Dear Lord, Andrew! What happened to your face?"

Andrew was pouring himself a cup of coffee when his parents walked into the kitchen. He'd managed to avoid them last night, but unfortunately that meant that his face now looked worse, even if it felt better this morning.

"Looks like you took a solid punch. I hope there's a good story," said his father. Count on Dad to be unconcerned that Andrew might have been in a bar brawl.

"It is a good story, although I don't come out looking too manly for this particular one. You two wanna sit down?"

"What kind of story is this?" asked his mother. "Oh, Honey, I don't know if I can take a sitting down story this morning. Not with the funeral and all." Andrew thought his mom had always had a flare for the dramatic. It's probably why she and his dad had used to fight so much.

"Mom, it's a quick story. The nutshell version, at least. You can get the long story when you feel more up to it." He proceeded to tell them that he'd managed to fall in love this summer, and was going to marry her. He didn't mention that he'd already proposed, but that could wait until he gave them the long version. He did say that she was slightly older than he and that she had kids. The son had punched him, by mistake, naturally. It was entirely the truth. Sugar-coated a bit, but they got the picture. They wouldn't expect a young girl when he introduced them, and they knew she was coming with a ready-made family. His mom cooed. She couldn't wait to meet the boys. And Andrew's new love, of course. She floated out the door, happy her son was finally going to settle down.

His dad wasn't quite so eager to swallow the sugar-coating. "How old are these boys? No ten-year-old leaves bruises like that."

"He's twenty-four and as big as an ox. Dad, don't tell Mom yet, okay? You'll meet Jenny today at the funeral. You might remember her. I was friends with her older son Josh in school. Trust me, we've been over this age gap thing more than I care to say. But she's The One, I know it. I'm gonna marry her, and I would rather do it with your blessing."

"Andrew, you're old enough to know your mind. Of course you have our blessing. Your mother might have some qualms at first, but she'll come around." His dad smiled and looked thoughtful then said, "Love comes in many forms, in unexpected ways. I'm glad you've found it." He slapped Andrew on the back and wandered off to get dressed.

Ryan paced the floor in agitation. "Mom, how long have you been seeing him? Do you even really know him? I mean, sure he was a nice guy in high school, but it's been ten years, and what's he done for himself? Not much, by the looks of it. I love you, but jeez, I thought you were looking for Mr. Right, not a Mr. Right Now. Let me talk to Aunt Karen. I bet she knows people. Or what about those internet dating sites? There are places that will have the kind of man you need, steady and dependable and–"

"Ryan, shut up. I do not need this right now. Do you hear yourself? Could you *possibly* be more insulting? I am a grown woman, and I know exactly what I want. Andrew–"

"Mom, I saw. For the love of God, don't spell it out! You think now Dad's gone, you'll have the fun you missed out on when you were young? Screwing the *lawnboy*? Dad deserves better than that. Treat his memory with a little respect! And *him* – I should have beaten him to a pulp for daring to touch you! You have no idea how pervy boys are. He probably wanted to do you then, and is laughing that he's got you on your back now!" His tirade was silenced with a furious slap to his cheek.

"Out. Get *out* of my house. Do not ever speak to me that way again! I don't want to see you unless you're back to apologize. I am your *mother*! You don't get to tell me how to live my life. I will do as I see fit, and as for you, get your mind out of the gutter! You have a lot of nerve. If your father were here, he'd knock you into next week for what you just said. Get out."

Jenny held her composure until he stomped out of the house. She didn't have time to dissolve into tears, but they came anyway. She heard him peel out of the driveway – *God, keep him safe!* She didn't know where he'd go, though she hoped it'd be to Karen's. She'd call him later. Right now, she had a day to get through, a funeral to get ready for and a damn party to put on. The day was off to a rip-roaring start. It couldn't possibly get any worse.

"That's the woman you want to marry? She seemed cold. Pretty enough, but not very friendly. You could do better; I can set you up –"

"Shut up." Andrew cut off his sister's catty remarks tersely. The initial introduction hadn't gone very well. A funeral had probably been the worst place to have it. His mother and sisters had been cold, too, which hadn't done much to put Jenny at ease. She'd been edgy to begin with, and the funeral struck familiar chords in her that she hadn't anticipated. His father, though, God bless him, had been warm and accepting. Of course, he'd known that Jenny was his age – or nearly so. Mom hadn't known. He probably should have told his family, after all. He could see the speculation in their eyes once they'd realized that his Jenny wasn't some young divorcee, but a mature woman with grown children. They wondered what she'd done to bewitch him, or what was wrong with her that she couldn't catch a man her own age. Andrew had a black eye because of her. Which begged the question: why in the world was she worth fighting over?

"Hey, I'm here. What do you need done first?" Andrew strode into the kitchen ready to work and put his sister's comments out of his mind. He wanted nothing more than to relax with a cold beer in hand and Jenny at his side, but he knew tonight wouldn't be that simple. He was determined, though, that the families would accept them, and that meant firmly sticking together. He wasn't going to back off just because the boys – *When did I start thinking of them as the boys?* – were being churlish. Or, to be fair, Ryan. He still didn't know what Josh thought, but he'd know soon enough. He wouldn't disappoint Jenny this time. She was his, and he'd fight for her, even if it meant alienating his friend. He wouldn't allow Jenny to be cowed, by either family.

She put him to work immediately, sending him off to the store for last-minute drinks and ice.

Jenny couldn't wait for the evening to be over already. Ryan had stormed off after being ordered out, and there was no sign of him. He didn't answer her phone calls, he wasn't at Karen's and no one had seen him. The funeral had been nice, but had dredged up all these emotions she didn't have time to deal with. His family hated her, or at least the women did. Now she had to tell her other son that she was marrying Andrew. She'd thought it couldn't get worse this morning with Ryan, but she'd been proven wrong. Surely things would start looking up tonight. She just might lose it if they didn't.

She heard a car pull into the drive. *Here goes nothing…*

Jenny greeted her son and future daughter-in-law at the door with a huge smile.

"Josh, hug your mother. Emily, it's so good to see you again. Are you excited about the move? Nervous? Oh, of course you are! Silly question! Sorry. I babble when I'm nervous. Yes, I'm nervous too! My baby's moving!" Jenny stopped for a second to breathe and Josh jumped into the conversation.

"Ma, where's Ryan? He said he had something important to tell me. Wanted to talk before the party got underway."

The forced cheerfulness Jenny had greeted them with fell away and the worry she felt for Ryan was readily apparent in her face as she answered. "He's gone. I don't know where, and I didn't ask. Come in and sit down please."

"Uh, okay. Bad news?" Josh reached for Emily's hand and grasped it for reassurance, Jenny noticed. *A good sign. Does he even know he did that?*

"Oh, Sweetie, not bad news, not at all! But serious news. Good news! At least, I think so." Jenny settled into the cozy chair next to the sofa, and leaned in to start on her story. She reminded him of the day he'd come looking for her and the wonderful talk they'd had.

"I had meant to wait until tomorrow to tell you, but Ryan…I want everything out in the open, and hopefully you will be happy for me. Just as I am so happy for you! I am seeing someone. One of the men I told you about before. It's serious. Marriage serious. I love him. Really love him." She stopped, unsure how to continue.

Josh jumped right in, with reassurance and smiles, "Oh, Mom, I am so happy for you. Why wouldn't I be? Don't worry about Ryan. He'll be fine. Once he gets used to the idea --"

"I don't know, Sweetie. I don't think he wants to get used to it. He was angry and belligerent, and…" Jenny's voice lowered as she recalled his hateful words. "mean."

The kitchen door opened and a familiar voice called out, "Jenny, I'm back! Where do you want this stuff?"

Josh smiled, "Shoulda known you'd be the first one here, Bud. Always helping out when you can. Hey! Guess what? Mom's gettin' married!" Andrew walked into the room, sporting the shiner Ryan had given him, and laid a hand on the back of Jenny's chair. "What the hell happened to your face?" Josh asked.

"Uh, Ryan happened. I see we haven't gotten to the good part of the story yet."

Josh very quickly added up the parts he knew, and surmised the parts he didn't. This certainly explained why Ryan wanted to talk to him, and why Mom wanted to get the first word.

"Mom? I just realized you've left out a really important detail. You wanna give me a name? Who's the lucky guy?" Josh never took his eyes off Andrew, and his stomach tightened as he saw in his periphery that his mother stood and brought Andrew forward to link her arm with his. Andrew kept his gaze locked with Josh's, refusing to back down. His eyes hardened in challenge. Josh could be an intimidating man. He'd been that way on the football field as well as on the wrestling mat. Sheer size had a lot to do with it. But Andrew had a steel core, too. Once he made a stand, he never backed down. One of their coaches likened him to a rat terrier, Josh remembered. It's what had made him such a fierce competitor, even when he was smaller than the rest of the guys on the team. Smaller, not weaker.

Josh nodded, slowly, his acceptance of Andrew. "You're sure, Mama?"

"I'm sure. We're sure." She turned to look at Andrew and smiled. "We're sure of us but we weren't sure about you. Or Ryan. Not to mention his family! But yes. Yes, I'm sure."

Josh could see by the way she looked at Andrew, her eyes never wavering, and the softness in those eyes that she loved him, and they would make it work.

"Alright then. If you're sure, I'm sure. But…it's gonna be weird, really weird. I'll talk to Ryan but he's not going to like it. Although I guess he already knows. He'll get over it. Eventually."

Emily, who had been quiet the entire time, stood and hugged her soon-to-be mother-in-law, and whispered in her ear. "I knew. He looks at you, and you are his world. It was there the day we met. I am so happy for you!" Aloud, she said, "Joshua, come congratulate the happy couple. Your mama needs a hug."

Jenny pulled away with surprise. And then pulled her in for another hug. "Emily you are a delight! I am so glad you're joining the family." She released her with a laugh. At least something had gone well today. "Well, now that's settled, we have a party to get ready for. Let's see what's still on my list of things to do."

"Josh, I'm stealing your mother away for an hour. The party's in full swing, you know where everything is, and she is desperate for some quiet time. This has been an unexpectedly stressful weekend." Andrew had pulled his friend aside for just a second. "I'm taking her up to the cemetery. She likes to sit with your dad. If you need us, that's where we'll be."

"Hey, uh...you and Mom? It's going to take some getting used to. I mean, I guess it'd take getting used to no matter who it was, but... Jeez! We used to talk about girls together and stuff, you know?"

"Hey, no worries, man. I know. Trust me, Ryan made it perfectly clear I need to keep my hands off her around you." He touched a fingertip to his still-tender cheek. At least his eye hadn't swollen shut. "I think he'd like me to keep my eyes off her, too. You know, we didn't plan this. It just happened, and I hope we can still get along and get past this awkward stage soon."

"It's okay, Bud, just, can you ease into any PDA with her over, say, the next five years or so? Give us a chance to get used to it."

"Deal! Okay, well, we'll be back in an hour."

Andrew collected Jenny and their jackets and walked with her into the fading light to the edge of town. They didn't talk much, which was alright with Andrew. He was rehearsing a speech in his head.

As they reached the bench where she always sat, she pulled him next to her and held his hand tight.

"Didn't you wanna talk to David? A lot's happened the past few days. I can go wander..."

"No, not now. Besides, I wanted David to meet you. Oh, that sounds ridiculous." She shook her head and dropped it into her hands. How silly was it to want to introduce your dead husband to your fiancé?

"Oh, Jenny Love, it's not so ridiculous. I like to run here, and I see people talking to their loved ones all the time. It's how we cope with death I guess. Heck, I used to come talk to Gramps, too. And I…I came here once to talk to David about you. To ask him for you. Does that sound crazy?" He hadn't planned to admit that – ever – but for Jenny he would.

Jenny smiled tenderly. "Oh Sweetheart, that doesn't sound crazy at all."

"Now that we're here, though, wanna tell me what happened with Ryan? You were pretty upset when I picked you up this morning, and I know it wasn't just the funeral," said Andrew.

"I don't want to talk about it. He was pretty hateful. I told him not to come back until he was ready to apologize. But, Andrew, he's my baby! Even though I told him to go, I worry. He was so angry. I hope he's okay. I don't know where he is. I just hope Josh is right and he'll come around. He doesn't even know we're getting married. He thinks you're just…he thinks we're only…" She couldn't even say it. That anyone would think that of either of them hurt, but the fact that her son would think it was humiliating.

"Jenny Love, it's gonna be okay. He'll call tomorrow, and we'll tell him then. He'll come around, I know he will. It just takes time." Andrew hoped he was right. Ryan had always been a hot-headed guy, but he was usually quick to cool down, too. This was a little different than a schoolyard scuffle, though. This was his mom, and Ryan was, if possible, the most protective son he'd ever met

"Hey, look at me, Sweetheart." Andrew reached into his pocket and pulled out the ring he'd been itching to give her. He held it up so she could see. In only the light of streetlamps, it still had a pleasing glint. "This was my grandmother's ring. She wanted me to give it to my bride, and she hoped my wife would get to wear it as long as she did. Sweet Jenny, I love you. You are my life and my world. Will you marry me?"

Jenny nodded. She was too overcome to say anything without it coming out a squeak. She held out her hand and let him slide the ring into place. Then she slid into his arms. "Andrew, I am so glad there's you." Her happiness and her heartache overcame her and the tears flowed again.

Andrew pulled her onto his lap and kissed her lips, cheeks, eyes and nose, gently and sweetly, and just a bit playfully, snuggling his face into the crook of her neck. He was ecstatic his Jenny was wearing his ring! He felt part caveman, part cowboy, part conquering hero. He grinned and gave in to the joy he felt. Surging to his feet, arms still tightly holding his Jenny, he swung her around in circles. She was so surprised she tightened her arms further and shrieked to be put down. Whoops and shrieks of laughter ensued, until they came to their senses, and he set her feet on the ground. Still giggling, she reached up and pecked his cheek.

Andrew grinned again and kissed her gently on the mouth. He quietly murmured into her ear, *"Say I'm weary, say I'm sad; Say that health and wealth have missed me; Say I'm growing old, but add - Jenny kissed me!"*

He swung her around in a slow circle and put her down, ready to walk back home.

Jenny walked in a daze. *Surely he couldn't know. How could he know that's what David used to say? He couldn't!*

"When did you start reading poetry? Have you always loved it?" She'd gotten her wits back together, and was curious. It wasn't unheard of for people to read poetry, of course. Lots of people did. Millions, even. It's just that she'd never really gotten the hang of it, and it struck her as interesting that both men she'd fallen in love with had poet's souls.

"Huh. I guess I started in high school. Yeah, English. We had to read Shakespeare, you know, and his sonnets were part of the course. I didn't get it at the time. But..." He stopped in his tracks. "I forgot. How could I forget something so huge? Jeez! I didn't get it, Shakespeare I mean, but one day I was complaining about our reading assignment to Josh, and Mr. Martin – David – overheard.

He explained the sonnet, and suggested a few other poets to read, ones that used more understandable English. Said to start with them, then go back to the Shakespeare. That maybe I'd understand better if I had a better grasp of the language, backing into Elizabethan style from the modern period. And he was right. I understood it, and I loved it. He's the one that encouraged it."

Jenny didn't know what to say. Nothing, she supposed. What did it matter in the long run? It's not like David groomed his successor by teaching him to love poetry. He hadn't planned to *have* a successor! It was a coincidence and nothing more. Other than that, they didn't seem to have a whole lot in common, certainly not physically. David had been a giant next to her and Andrew was only a little bit taller. If David was built like a Clydesdale, Andrew was more like a Mustang. David had had dark brown hair and brown eyes, and Andrew was fair with blue eyes. David thrived on a busy schedule, constantly working and doing. Andrew took time to relax. David had been outspoken, while Andrew was quiet. They were opposites in so many ways. But they both loved to laugh. They had playful boyish sides she knew they only showed to her. They were thoughtful and kind, putting others before themselves. They were intelligent, with poet's souls. And they both loved her. She was very lucky, indeed.

Once back at the house, the business of the party took priority once again, and they had no time to talk. They shared glances and smiles, and Jenny took every opportunity to covertly admire the new ring she wore. It was beautiful, in an old-fashioned way, and it fit her perfectly, her hand *and* her personality. She would have loved to meet his grandmother.

Chapter 25

"I'm thinking, if it's okay with you, that is, that we should have a quiet ceremony, just family and a few close friends. Would you mind?" Jenny wanted nothing more than to elope, just the two of them, but she figured Karen might never forgive her. And the sooner the better. Now that she'd found love again, she was even more impatient in her middle age than she'd been when she was young.

"Do I look like I mind? I'd marry you tomorrow morning in work clothes. I don't need the fancy suit, or the flowers, or three hundred of our closest acquaintances. I just need you and a preacher."

It had been a week since the funeral, the going-away party and lunch with his parents. Lunch had been so much nicer than the initial meeting, partly because his catty sisters hadn't been invited, and his mother had warmed to Jenny almost right away without their influence. She and Jenny had been able to talk and laugh, and discover a kindred love of the feminine things in life. Both Andrew's parents had seen why Jenny completely captured his heart. They'd been pleased, too, to see Grandma's ring on her finger. Pleased that she was wearing it with pride, and impressed that she wasn't fussy and insistent upon a 'new' ring.

"Do you have a time-frame in mind?" Andrew prodded. "Tomorrow? Next week? I am willing to wait until next month, but I draw the line at next year. I cannot possibly wait until then." Andrew grabbed her around the waist and nuzzled her ear. He was doing everything he could to tempt her into a more immediate date. She had a weakness for neck-nuzzling, and he felt her melt just a little bit more. "I'll call the preacher and see what we can do. I vote for this evening. Can you work that into your schedule?"

Jenny was weak-kneed and loving it. She stroked her hands over his shoulders and down his back. "Oh – I can't tonight. I promised Karen we'd meet for dinner and shopping. I need a new dress to get married in, you know. She insists. But really and truly, when?"

"November," Andrew told her. "Thanksgiving. It's a whole month, and time will fly. Just our families, and Karen and Danny. And Mrs. Petersen, if that's alright. She's like a grandmother to me, and I think she'd love to come."

"Of course it's alright. She's family to you. I guess I'd better get started on invitations." Jenny smiled softly. She was getting married. And then she grinned. She was getting *married*!

"This gown is perfect! It almost matches your eyes, it's just a bit duskier. Try it!"

Jenny rolled her eyes. She'd been looking for a pink dress, or rosy. But she tried the one her friend held out to her anyway. Perfect! Karen was her good luck charm!

"What should I do for invitations?" She wanted to have them printed and engraved. It might be her second wedding, but it was Andrew's first (and only, she sincerely hoped!). She wasn't *that* much older than him. Even though she only had a month, she wanted the details to be as carefully planned as possible.

"Don't you worry," Karen said. "I have it all taken care of. I want to do this for you. Please let me! I don't have any girls to manage weddings for. You're the only chance I have to plan one!" Karen looked and sounded so melodramatic that Jenny had to laugh and acquiesce. It was good to have her friend helping and keeping her occupied. Jenny wasn't sure she'd last four weeks without Andrew in her bed. She could barely wait until their wedding night. Every time they were together, the tension was thick enough to cut. And his kisses, she was sure he tempted her on purpose. She wasn't going to give in though, at least, that's what she had to keep telling herself. *Twenty-eight more days…*

"Ryan won't answer my calls. He was so angry. I was hoping he'd be happy for me. He said he would be."

It was two weeks until the wedding, and Ryan hadn't called or texted, or answered her calls, since he'd left before Josh's party. Karen was just about to call the boy herself and give him a piece of her mind. He was acting like a child. If David were here, none of this would be happening, because David wouldn't tolerate this for a minute. Jenny was being too soft on him.

"He'll come around. He will. Don't worry. If I have to drive up there myself and drag him back by the ear, he will be here to give you away. Okay?" Karen reassured her friend as best she could, and took a mental note to call Josh. Josh had always been able to talk sense into his hot-headed little brother.

Josh sat listening to the phone ring until Ryan's voice-mail picked up. "Dude, what the hell? Pick up the phone and call me. If I have to drive up there to kick your ass, you can bet I will. You might be bigger than me, but you're still my little brother. You're being a jackass and you know it. Call me back." Josh left his message and called Aunt Karen back.

"I don't know what's up with him. I know he's always been super-protective of Mom, but this is stupid. I can't figure it out. At first I thought it was just that she's getting remarried. Then I thought it was because of *who* she's marrying, but he used to like Andrew just as much as anyone. So, hell if I know. How's Mom doing? Holding up under the stress of planning? Emily has moments of panic trying to get ready by June!" Josh knew that Karen was taking care of most of it anyway, but there was still a lot to be done. Stuff the guys weren't clued into mostly. He'd be perfectly happy if Em said they were eloping to Vegas, just to avoid the stress. Though their mothers would likely feel deprived of the big event.

"She's fine, except for worrying over Ryan. If that boy doesn't show up, I will kill him. Okay. Thank you, Josh. Let me know if you talk to him. Love you. Bye."

Chapter 26

Ryan had gotten every one of the text messages and voicemails from his family, and with each one he felt worse and more awkward about calling back. He wasn't angry. Not anymore, at least, but he was ashamed. He had said awful things. He'd been so wrapped up in his own world, wanting everything to be just so. For him, it was as if time stood still; he still felt the way he'd felt when Dad had died. He was in shock, angry and bewildered. How could Dad be gone? Dad had been invincible, or so he'd thought. Sometimes Ryan still couldn't quite grasp that he was dead. Sometimes when he went home, he drove on autopilot to the house he'd grown up in, expecting Dad to greet him on the front porch. When he realized his mistake and headed to his mom's house instead, the sadness would settle in his gut. He'd drive around until he had it back under wraps, and show up to Mom's all smiles. She didn't know. How could she know that he wasn't coping? He should be. *They* had – Josh, Mom, even Karen and Danny, they were all doing alright, more than alright. They were doing just fine without Dad. As that thought ate at him, the anger settled in once more. How could they forget him so soon?

He heard a car door shut and glanced out the window. He was shocked to see a beat up old truck in the drive and a determined looking Andrew walking up to the front door. *Shit…*

Ryan opened the door and stood aside, silently inviting his guest in. He could tell by the look in Andrew's eye that he was in a heap of trouble. Had he come on his own, or had Karen or Josh sent him? He knew his mom wouldn't have. She'd just quietly wait for him to come back in his own time, just like she always did. Ugh…he really was such a jackass*! Just like Josh said…*

"Before you lay into me," Ryan started, "I'm sorry. I know why you're here. Josh called again this morning. Mom must really be in a state. He's threatening to kick my ass."

"Good for him. I'll do it now if I have to. Save him the trouble. I'm pretty sure I owe you a thrashing for nearly killing me last time I saw you anyway." Andrew was pissed, and a simple 'I'm sorry' wasn't going to cut it. Ryan hadn't had to watch Jenny deal with her bewildered hurt. She might be Ryan's mom, but she was going to be *his* wife, and damned if he was going to let anyone hurt her like that, son or no.

"I said I was sorry. How was I supposed to know you were there by invitation? I don't know why it's such a big deal." He was feeling hot-headed and more defensive by the minute.

"It's not a big deal. I would've done the same thing. Whatever you said to your mother, however, is another story altogether. She won't tell me exactly what you said, which is probably a good thing for you. You left without saying goodbye to her, and you haven't talked to her since. We're set to get married in a week, and she wants you to be there. She says you're mad at her, and she doesn't know why. She's sure you're mad because she's getting married. Either you don't like me, or you don't like her getting married at all, no matter who it is.

Is that it? You want her to spend the rest of her life pining away for your dad? Forty or fifty years alone, you want her to do that? Do you think that's fair? Do you think your dad would want that for her?" Andrew's voice had become harder by the second. He hadn't realized he was so angry at Ryan, and it had nothing to do with the punch thrown. Everything to do with Jenny's hurt.

Ryan's back was up again, and even though Andrew was right, all the rage he'd been feeling was bubbling over. "Don't talk to me about what my dad would or wouldn't want. You didn't know him like I did, you weren't his son! He'd for damn sure want better for her than a runt like you. What do you even do for a living? You dig in the dirt and scrape by on odd jobs; I can see that by the rust-bucket you drive. You see Mom as easy pickins? A rich sugar mama to keep you warm? You son of a bitch! Just thinking of you with her makes me want to puke. You're not even half the man Dad was. You don't deserve her. She should be with Dad. I should do everyone a favor and lay you out!" Ryan didn't think anymore, just swung.

Andrew was prepared this time, though. He could see Ryan working himself up, and he remembered all his fighting moves. Andrew ducked and turned, catching Ryan with his own tricks. Ryan was on the floor before he knew what hit him, and Andrew had him locked in an arm bar, threatening to break it if he didn't settle down. *Damn...I forgot how quick he was. For a runt.*

"Do not *ever* talk about your mother that way to me. She is not some stupid slut I'm using for what I can get out of her. She's going to be my *wife*, and I won't have anyone disrespecting her. Got it?" He tightened his hold and stretched Ryan's arm. "I oughta break it just to spite you. Here she is worried about *you,* wondering how *you* are, and all you can do is bad-mouth her and pick a fight. A fight you're not going to win. She can't be with your dad, you idiot. Or did you forget that he's gone? He's not coming back. She's not some heartless bitch who moved on because she was tired of the current model. He *died* for Chrissakes. You are a fucking idiot to think anything else."

"Of course I know he's dead." Ryan said at last. "Who do you think found him? Fuck you! Get off me." Ryan bucked, but it made his arm pull. Like a dog with a bone, Andrew wouldn't let up until he was good and ready. *Son of a bitch…*

Andrew *hadn't* known. He didn't really know any of the details of David's death. He hadn't asked at the time, and he'd never wanted to bring it up after. He only knew David had had a stroke or aneurism or something…

"Say you'll come to the wedding."

"Fine – fine! I'll be there! Now get off me!"

"You won't just be there. You'll be there with a smile on that ugly face, and you'll walk her down the aisle. If I have to come get you Friday night, your face is going to get even uglier – do you understand me? If you know what's good for you, you'll come Thursday for Thanksgiving dinner with the whole damn family, too.

When I get home I want to hear that you've called Jenny with the happy news. Got it?" Andrew released Ryan's arm; it was going to be sore for a while. He was just grateful he hadn't accidentally broken it. Andrew stood and held out a hand to help Ryan up, but he ignored it.

Ryan stood and brushed himself off and noticed Brent, dumbfounded in the doorway. *Dammit…*

"Uhhh…I'm Brent…Ryan's roommate…" Brent was not sure at all what to think. He had never seen Ryan in a fight before. He was so big that most people backed off and let Ryan have his way, and he'd never imagined that if Ryan *were* in a fight, he'd land on the bottom, much less lose to a guy half his size.

"I'm Andrew and I was just leaving. Can you make sure Ryan heads back home for the holiday? His mom misses him."

"Uh-huh." Brent walked him to the door and closed it slowly behind him.

"Mind telling me what that was all about?" Brent's question was as nonchalant as possible.

"Bite me. That," Ryan gave a snort of disgust, "was my mother's boyfriend." *Fiancé. Whatever.* He wasn't used to being bested by scrawny runts. His pride was hurt, and he was still angry. He hated knowing that Andrew was right – he was being a complete tool, and stubbornly refusing to do what he knew was right. Andrew was a good guy – always had been. Ryan had used to look up to him, even. He wasn't taking advantage of Mom, and Ryan knew it. It was just hard missing his dad, and he wasn't ready for the changes he knew were coming. Ryan shut himself in his room for the rest of the day to cool down and think. And to call his mother. He was hesitant to test whether Andrew might actually break his arm or his face – the scrawny runt was strong!

"Mom, it's me, Ryan. I'm sorry I haven't called. I wanted to let you know I'll be down for Thanksgiving, if that's still okay. Can I come Wednesday night? I'll stay through the weekend. I'm sure Karen has room if the house is already full. Love you. See you in a couple days." Ryan hung up the phone, profoundly grateful he could just leave a message. Hopefully that would suffice.

Andrew was troubled his whole drive home. He contemplated Ryan's words, knowing full well they were spoken in anger. Nonetheless they pierced close to the heart, hit at his deepest insecurity. He did feel unworthy of Jenny sometimes. She never made him feel that way. Yet, the reality was that he would never be rich. That's not the kind of job he had. He paid his bills, and had enough for a few extras, but his means didn't go far beyond that. He guessed that Mr. Martin would have kept Jenny very comfortable, and he knew that Robert would have done that and more.

Andrew was old-fashioned. He wanted to be able to take care of his family – Jenny – without her having to work if she didn't want to. She would probably always have to, truth be told. The fact that she liked her job and *wanted* to work, he supposed that was a blessing.

Mr. Martin had always been a man larger than life. He seemed like he just had it all perfectly together. How could Andrew possibly live up to that? He was going to screw up. He forgot his own mother's birthday sometimes, eventually it would happen with his wife, too. Or he would say or do something that would unintentionally hurt her. He didn't even want to think about it. It made his stomach tighten in knots, just remembering how he'd hurt before, and he never wanted to do it again.

Andrew pulled into the driveway. He'd promised to be home for dinner, and he'd made it just in time.

"Ryan finally called." Jenny said as Andrew came inside. "He left a message. He's coming down

Wednesday night, and staying through the weekend. He'll be here for the wedding. You don't know anything about that, do you?"

"I know Karen and Josh have been calling him every day for the past two weeks. One of them probably got through to him. Josh most likely. What are you making for dinner? It smells great in here!" He kissed her cheek and walked to the fridge for a drink. He didn't want to talk about his trip. He hadn't intended to keep it from her when he went, but he was slightly embarrassed that he had gone at all, and that he'd bullied his soon-to-be step-son into coming for the wedding. He shouldn't have had to. In an odd way, he was glad he had. Something Ryan had said still stuck in his memory. Ryan was still hurting – *really* hurting – over the loss of his dad. It was yet one more thing Jenny and he needed to sort through before the week was out.

"You've been quiet tonight. Penny for your thoughts?" Jenny wanted to tease Andrew out of this mood. They would be married a week from today, and he seemed a little distant, too distant for her taste. He'd gone off on some secret errand, and come home rather melancholy. "Sweetheart, we're supposed to share our troubles as well as our joy. What's wrong? Can I help? I know I can at least listen." She snuggled into him as they sat on the sofa. At the very least, she could offer her touch.

"Jenny, do you ever…?" He had no idea how to say what he was thinking. How could he ask her if she wished she still had David? He knew that on some level she did, but she probably wouldn't say so because that would mean they wouldn't be together. She was always sensitive to others' feelings. She wouldn't want to hurt him. "What I mean is, do you ever compare me to David? I can't compete with him, I can't give you everything he could have, and…are you sure you want to be with me?"

"Oh, Andrew, Sweetheart, you think you don't live up to the memory of this giant of a man that everyone has put on a pedestal now that he's gone? Oh, Love – no. I have done you a disservice by not mentioning this earlier, but by God, David was *not* perfect! He was wonderful, and I loved him, but he made his share of mistakes, just like we all do, and you cannot compare yourself to him! He was just as human as the rest of us." Jenny was dismayed that he'd been worried over this and she hadn't realized. It should have occurred to her when Andrew mentioned in the letter he wrote that he'd thought David was 'damn near perfect' – or was he referring to Robert? Either way, he was wrong, and she wouldn't have it.

"It's just that he was so smart, successful, and he could give you anything. I'm..."

"You are smart and successful, too! I don't measure success by your bank account, Sweetheart. You should know that by now. You are doing what you love, you're helping people, and you make a difference every day. That's success. Did David have that? Yes. In a different way and a completely different industry, an industry that required him to work long hours, and was stressful and frustrating sometimes. But he loved it, he thrived on it.

I'll tell you a secret. Sometimes, I hated it. I wanted him to be home with us, and he was on a plane halfway across the country. When he *was* home, though, we were his world, and I know it. He loved his job, yes, but he loved us more, and he worked so hard for *us*. I tried not to complain, even when I hated it. Now that I'm older he would have been home more, I suppose. I like that you can be here. Your job is here, not in nine different offices across the country. I *love* that. Call me selfish, but I'm glad you do what you do. I'm glad you come home every night." She studied his face and raised an arm to run her fingers through his hair, trying to sooth away the worry and tension she saw.

"What about all the shows and museums and things that you liked to do with Robert? I don't do that. I can't afford it, and those things don't really interest me anyway. You could go with Karen if you want, but..."

"That *I* liked to do? That Karen! I should have corrected that impression, too. Sure, I like it sometimes, but every weekend? No, thank you. I am a homebody. I like shopping, it's true, but I was beginning to get exhausted going out all the time with Robert. He couldn't sit still!" Jenny chuckled. "I don't think he liked being quiet very much, and I love it."

She scooted up onto his lap and snuggled closer, straddling him so they faced each other. "Look, don't we fit together perfectly? You are my ideal match." She kissed him, and while she kissed him she twisted this way and that, fitting herself perfectly to him. All her wriggling, she knew, was heating him up, just as it was heating her. It was only a week more, but she wanted a great deal more than kisses tonight. Just as she reassured him that he was loved exactly as he was, for who he was, she needed a bit of reassurance, too. Reassurance that he found her to be just as attractive in body as he found her mind and heart. That he loved every inch of her imperfect, aging self. She was too shy to say so, however, not outright, not in this moment.

"You're making it very difficult for me to keep my hands off you." His hands were skimming over her torso as he relished the kisses she scattered over his face and neck. "Jenny my love – I thought we were going to wait it out. I don't know if I can do that if you keep this up." Andrew felt powerless beneath her. She was so beautiful, and she was all his. Or would be, in a week. But the things she was doing with her mouth…oh sweet Lord, he couldn't think straight. Surely a week either way wouldn't matter.

No, it *did* matter, he argued with himself. He wanted to honor her, and she had said she wanted to wait. They would wait, even if it killed him, which it might. Andrew thought he might explode. He was hard as a rock, and had been for weeks. Everything hurt, and the only cure was Jenny. Cold showers only went so far, and he'd need an ice bath tonight. He shuddered at the thought.

Andrew pulled her arms from around him. "We have to stop. Do you want me to ravage you right here on the sofa? You deserve better than that! Sweetheart, I don't want you to regret anything. If you want to wait, we'll wait, even if it kills me. You're so hot. My blood boils just thinking about being with you." At least, that's what he thought he said. It could have come out differently, because the look on her face reflected only hurt and disappointment. Had he said something wrong? How had that happened? *Dammit…was she crying? For the love of God…*

"Jenny, what did I say? Tell me what I did!" He was thoroughly confused and he was a little hazy with lust, so his brain wasn't working right anyway, but surely trying to be a gentleman was a good thing. Wasn't it? As soon as he had blood back in his skull, he'd be able to work it out.

Jenny hadn't meant to cry. Perhaps it was just the stress of the past month and the coming week hitting her all of a sudden. She knew she was probably being irrational – but he was resisting her! He was supposed to find her *irresistible*! He'd said so, yet nobody was ravishing anyone. She pushed herself away from him and ran to her room. She was being ridiculous, and she knew it, which only made her feel worse. Andrew loved her and that's all that mattered. So why couldn't she stop crying? She hated crying; she always ended up looking like a beet.

Andrew might be hazy, but he wasn't stupid. He followed her to her room, only to find her sobbing into her pillow. He crawled up onto the bed and stretched out beside her. He didn't talk, just wrapped her up in his arms and held her while she cried. At least she'd dampened his raging lust for the moment.

"You gonna tell me what's wrong? I thought I was being an honorable gentleman. But if you want me to be a horndog, I can do that." He placed a hand over her breast and squeezed. He felt, rather than heard, her chuckle.

"It's stupid. I can't tell you. You'll think I'm being silly."

"It's not stupid if it matters to you. Besides, you never cry over silly things. You can tell me, Sweetheart."

"Promise you won't laugh. Or roll your eyes. Or say I'm being silly."

"I promise – cross my heart." He crossed his heart, and leaned up on an elbow to see her better. "Tell me."

Jenny turned over on her side to face him. Then found that she couldn't face him. *This is embarrassing!* She focused her eyes on his chest and confessed, "I want you to think I'm irresistible. But you did a fine job of resisting me. I want you to think I'm pretty. All of me, even the parts I don't like."

"Jenny, if you think I don't find you irresistible, you might be a little bit crazy." He grabbed her hand and placed it over his crotch. "That is what you do to me. God, Jenny, I'm living this month with a constant hard-on, waiting for Saturday! I want to ravish you daily. I'm twenty-seven, long past my prime, and I'm not getting any younger, you know." He smiled at his own joke. "But my mind is stronger. You set limits, and I'm trying to live by them. You want to know how much I want you? How much I love your lips, your eyes, your hands and feet, hips and breasts? I could go on and on and on..." Andrew moved down so he could kiss her toes and began to kiss every inch of her, with a running monologue on the beauty of each of her parts. He edged up the hem of her dress, only exposing her flesh as he reflected on its charms. Jenny decided that being undressed by inches might be the most erotic thing ever. By the time he'd reached her hips, she'd stopped smiling and had thrown back her head, twisting her hands in the sheets, writhing in pleasure at the special attention he gave to the area.

He kissed his way up to her tantalizing breasts. They were the most perfect part of her, if he had to choose one thing. And her hands. Her hands were magical. Her touch set him on fire.

By the time he reached her face he was drenched in sweat. The effort it took not to plunge into her and relieve his own want was too much.

"How can I describe your beautiful face? Jenny, my love, this face will always be beautiful, ever more beautiful as we grow old together. Your thick dark hair might lighten over time, but I will never tire of burying my face in it, feeling the silk of it." Andrew stared intently into her eyes.

"Now do you believe I find you beautiful? That you are and always will be irresistible to me? Do you see the effort it takes me not to have my way with you? It will be like this the rest of our lives. But please, please, Jenny! Don't ever torture me this way again." Andrew flopped over on his back and covered his face with his arms.

Jenny was speechless. He had made love to her – all of her – and taken no pleasure for himself, except that which he derived from pleasing her. He gave too much, and asked nothing in return. She couldn't let it stand.

She could see him outlined clearly against the denim of his jeans as she reached gingerly toward his zipper. She'd barely touched it, though, before his hand shot out to stop her. "Please, Jenny – just let it go." He would be mortified if she continued.

"But Andrew, why should you suffer? I was wrong, and I'm sorry, and I want you to have what I did."

His grip was firm. "No, not tonight. I will wait."

"Now who's being silly? You don't need…oh…

Oh." There was a damp spot seeping through where her fingers had pressed.

"Believe me now? You don't even have to touch me."

He kept his face covered, still trying to find his equilibrium. She completely undid him. He only hoped it would get easier to bear over the years.

Jenny insisted on removing his clothes and bringing a hot cloth to sooth him. Then she tucked them both into bed and curled around him to sleep. Sleeping didn't break the rule she'd set, and she wanted to be with him tonight. She wanted to be with him every night.

It was Wednesday already, and there was still so much to be done for tomorrow and for Saturday. Jenny stood in her kitchen sipping her morning coffee, going over her mental to-do list one more time. She felt almost as though she hadn't left it in days! When she was at work, all she could think of was her to-do list, and she moved through her job on auto-pilot. She was baking and cooking as much as she could ahead of time for all the big meals coming up.

Thank God she had Karen to help her and to keep her busy. After her encounter with Andrew Saturday night, she'd tried to keep a bit of physical distance from him. She felt guilty about testing him, and even more guilty about the frisson of pleasure that shot through her to know – really *know* – that he found her beautiful. Not "beautiful for a woman her age," or "because she was beautiful on the inside." He thought she was beautiful, stunning, ravishing, gorgeous, period. No qualifiers. He'd told her to no end, but she'd been too stubborn to believe. It had taken his stubbornness to show her this truth.

Chapter 27

Her boys would both be here sometime tonight. Just as she wondered when and who would be first, the door opened. Ryan stood there, all six feet four inches of him, still looking for all the world like a little boy lost. Jenny knew she had told him to leave, that she should still be angry (and she *did* still expect an apology) but she was so glad to see him! She met him where he stood and reached up to hug and kiss her son.

"Hey, Mom." He held on tight. His voice deserted him, so he just squeezed her tighter.

"Alright, alright, you're gonna squeeze the life out of me!" Her boys always hugged tighter when they couldn't find words. She'd wait, and they'd come.

"Go put your things in the guest room. You're staying with me. Aunt Karen is handling the others. Then come out here and we'll talk."

Ryan moved slowly. He didn't want to talk, but his counselor had said it needed to be done, and he knew in his gut that the doctor was right.

"I know it's cold, but can we go somewhere? Take a walk or something?" Ryan asked. He didn't want to be here in case someone else came, like Andrew, or even Josh. He needed privacy for this.

"Of course. Let me get my coat."

They left the house and walked down the road in silence. Ryan was troubled, searching for the words he'd rehearsed to say. Jenny let him think, content that he was here and glad that he'd come back.

"Mom, do you remember what it was like for you when dad first died?" He knew she did. It wasn't something one forgot, but it was a place to start the conversation.

"Yes, I remember. And I remember what it was like for you, too." Ryan had been devastated. They all were, but somehow Ryan had been beyond that. He'd been inconsolable. He had turned into himself that summer, and had lashed out at anyone who tried to pull him out of his grief, even for a moment. Yet as heart-wrenching as his grief had been, by the end of summer, he had seemed to be coming out of it. He had gone off to school with a smile, did well enough in his classes, and came home for winter break the same old Ryan he'd been before.

In his effort to express himself Ryan felt small again, young and unsure, but desperate for the understanding and forgiveness of his mother.

"Mama, you remember the side of me I wanted you to see, but, Mama, I…I miss Dad. Sometimes I still miss him like it was just last week. And I didn't want you to see that. I didn't want anyone to see that. Real men don't cry the way I did. After Dad died, I bawled like a baby anytime I knew I was absolutely alone. Once I went to school, I couldn't do that any longer, so I shoved it all down; I didn't want to feel it anymore. Instead, I pushed my friends away, numbed myself by drinking and getting into fights. I was pretty awful, actually, you just didn't see it, and when I came home, I'd put on a mask. Instead of dealing with Dad's death, I pretended it hadn't happened. It was working just fine for me until…until you said you were ready to move on. I know you wanted me to be happy for you, so I said I was. And I tried to be; I *wanted* to be. But Mama, I just couldn't understand how you'd be ready when I still hurt so much."

Jenny had latched onto his arm by this point, partly for warmth as they walked, but also to comfort him in some small way with her touch. She squeezed his arm with hers, silently urging him to go on.

"Mama, I'm so sorry I hurt you. I had no right. I…" Ryan fumbled for what to say next, struggling to apologize. Finding the right words was difficult.

"I saw a counselor on Monday." He continued. "It really hit me that I needed to. I don't like myself – how angry I get…and the doc said that it's pretty common – anger in grief, that is. I guess I didn't realize… but anyway… He's going to help me. I want to get better." Ryan wanted to tell his mom about Saturday, that Andrew was the motivation for seeing a counselor, but he didn't come out looking too good in that encounter, and with his bullying last month, he held off. He'd tell her another time.

"Oh, Honey, I wish I'd known. I'm sorry, too." She was. She'd never questioned that Ryan seemed to get over his dad's death so quickly, probably because she was so centered on her own grief. For all that she prided herself on her mothering skills, she'd really let him down on this front.

Ryan swallowed hard, and tried to choose his next words carefully. "Seeing you with…him…I was surprised, and I reacted. Poorly." *Ugh, that's an understatement!* "I'm so sorry. For my hurtful words, and for being such a complete jackass."

"Oh, Baby, it'll be alright. Thank you. But, you know, this thing with Andrew, it's not going away. He's not a passing fancy. We're getting *married*. He's a permanent part of the family now. You will have to accept that at some point." She wanted it to be now, for him to be happy for her, to accept this change and to embrace it right away. Though she knew it was unrealistic, she still wanted it.

"I know, Mama. Someday, just not yet." He cleared his throat and kept walking ahead. "I do want you to be happy. I know Dad would want you to be happy. I am glad you found…" He still had a hard time saying Andrew's name. It was too weird that they were together. "Yeah, well, I need time. I'll be there for the wedding, and I'll play nice. But I am not ready for this at all."

"As long as you are there, my day will be complete. I just want my boys with me." Jenny nudged him with her shoulder, and looked up at his face to catch his eye. He might outwardly be a giant, but she still saw the little boy he was on the inside.

They'd circled the blocks and were almost home again.

"Thanks Mom, for letting me come back, and for not hating me."

"Ryan! I could never – and *will* never – hate you. You're my baby!"

"About that. Think you could stop calling me Baby all the time? You're killing my street cred…" Ryan ventured a smile and a glance at his mom. They may not be completely okay, but they would be; he was content with that for now. If they could joke like they used to, maybe it'd get better faster.

Hey, Sugarbear. Just wanted to see you once more. I won't be coming around too much for a while. Not at all for a long time, I think.

I still love you. Don't ever think I don't! But I love him, too, and he deserves all of me, just like you did. I know how you guys think! If I come here to see you he'll worry that he's not doing something right, or that my love is divided, so I need to say goodbye again.

Jenny was surprised by how fresh her loss felt again. The realization was accompanied by sudden tears. While she was certain she was prepared for remarriage, and was looking forward to it in anticipation, this morning Jenny was overtaken by the reality that this wedding was going to change her life as much as her first one had, something she hadn't truly realized until now. She'd woken up this morning, and she'd felt the need to say goodbye, not just to David, but to who she had been. She'd been Mrs. David Martin for all of her adult life.

Tomorrow that name would be gone, and in a way, she felt that a part of herself would be gone as well. When he'd died her identity hadn't really changed, but tomorrow…tomorrow she would become Mrs. Andrew Sommers. She'd still be Jenny, but it was different, and it would take some getting used to. *Jenny Sommers. Mrs. Andrew Sommers.* Funny how something so obvious had escaped her. She'd been so preoccupied with Ryan she hadn't given it much thought.

Keep watching over us, especially Ryan. He needs you. Oh, David, he's still hurting, so much! I didn't know, and now that I do I'm just heartbroken for him. Josh, too. He misses you as much as we do, and he's farther away now. I'm not sure if that makes it better or worse. The boys will always miss you. They're always hoping you'll approve of what they do, and I try to let them know you'd be so proud, and I know you would be. You'd be so proud of our boys.

She needed to get going. There were things to be done for the rehearsal tonight. She kissed her hand and laid it on the stone. *Love ya, Sugarbear…love ya.* With that, Jenny made her way home.

Morning had dawned, bright and sunny and frosty cold. *A perfectly wonderful day for a wedding!* Jenny had stayed awake late into the night, but was still up with the sunrise. She felt like a little girl on Christmas morning, she was so excited! Emily and Karen helped her into her dress and loosely curled and pinned her hair. Andrew would be pleased to see it down. He always said he liked it best around her shoulders, though she hardly ever wore it that way.

The morning hours seemed to drag, until suddenly time flew, and it was time to go.

"Ready, Son?" Andrew's father was standing at his bedroom door, signaling that it was time to head to the chapel.

"Never been more ready for anything in my life." He slipped the ring he'd been holding into his breast pocket and headed out with his dad.

Andrew watched his lovely bride approach him with her sons, one on either side. *Was there ever a more beautiful sight?* They each placed a kiss on her cheek before Josh placed her hand in Andrew's.

Josh had agreed to stand as his best man, and Ryan stood with him as well, although Andrew hadn't asked. He had a feeling Josh had talked him into it, as a show of solidarity. Well, it made Jenny happy so he was happy, too. Her eyes were shining brightly, and she was smiling – smiling at him!

Jenny's eyes had locked onto Andrew the moment she'd stepped through the archway. He was handsome and dapper in his dark suit, but the twinkle in his eye was what drew her attention. That twinkle, and the secret smile. The smile that said he knew what she was thinking. And he did. Last night he'd given her another letter, in which he described everything he wanted to do with her once they were finally, *finally*, alone. It was almost all she could think about. She knew she'd have hours yet to wait, but it would be well worth it. He caught her eye during the homily and winked. Jenny blushed to realize her mind had wandered yet again. She focused her gaze on the book in the minister's hand, and focused her mind on the rest of the ceremony.

"You may now kiss your bride." The minister's words brought a grin to Andrew's face, and he savored the moment as he leaned toward his wife. To Jenny, the seconds he stood there grinning at her were too long to wait. She reached up and brought his lips to hers, only to hear him whisper into her mouth, "Jenny kissed me." She couldn't help herself – she laughed aloud and kissed him again, with arms thrown around him in carefree abandon. As Josh cleared his throat, she opened her eyes to see her two sons, slightly scandalized but none the worse for wear. She unwound her arms and they faced the applauding guests as the minister introduced Mr. and Mrs. Andrew Sommers.

Ryan stood to the side of the dance floor watching his mother with her new husband. He may not have been ready for her to remarry, but it was clear that they fit together very well. There was something there. Something he'd forgotten about in the years since his father's death – the sense of harmony. She'd had that with Dad, and it was good that she had it again. He could see it in Emily and Josh, too. The rightness of being with one's love. Ryan thought, perhaps, he'd almost had it once. *Maybe I'll find it again someday…*

Andrew and Jenny sat under the pergola late that night, staring through the slats at the clear starry sky. More accurately, Jenny was looking up. Andrew was staring at his bride.

"Have you ever seen anything so beautiful?" she asked.

"No. No, I haven't."

Jenny turned to look at him. "No, silly. I mean the stars." But she smiled anyway. "Winter stars are always brighter. Twinkling lights shining down, as if trying to make up for our lack of daylight. The moon is a lovely little sliver, like a sideways smile. Soon it'll be so big and brilliant we'll have to go for a midnight walk under it."

"That's fanciful talk tonight…and it'll be awfully cold for a midnight walk in December." As it was, they sat there, all their wedding finery covered up with parkas and blankets.

"You're right, it'll be cold, but I've got my love to keep me warm." She smiled up at the stars again, the tune to the old song running through her mind. Her memory stretched back to the summer nights spent in quiet companionship with the man who was now her husband. Her mind stretched forward to anticipate the coming years spent in the same chairs, with the same loving companionship, and more immediately, anticipating the loving he'd described in such pleasurable detail. Jenny pulled herself up out of her chair and made her way to the kitchen door. "I'm sure you promised me a great deal more than stargazing tonight. Are you going to sit here all alone or are you going to join me inside?"

"I thought you'd never ask!" Andrew was at her side in a moment. He opened the door, and before she could take a step, he swept her up into his arms and carried his Jenny Love over the threshold.

About the Author

April Bennett is a professional musician and teacher of singing. She lives in the heart of Ohio with her husband, two children, a spoiled dog, and two quirky turtles. As a life-long reader and late-blooming writer, she was thrilled to discover a love story taking shape inside her and insisting on being let loose.

Her favorite place on earth is on a beach in summer, with a good book in hand and the warm sun shining above the umbrella. For fun, April loves reading, walking, shopping, goofing off with her crazy family, and the occasional Netflix binge (with or without the crazy family).

This is her debut novel.

You can connect with April directly by email
aprilbennettbooks@gmail.com

or follow her on Twitter
@aprilbennettbks

Acknowledgements

Thank you to my parents, sister, and dear friends who fostered in me a love for the English language and reading. And to the hundreds of authors who fed my curious reading mind with their imaginations. I am doubly inspired now that I know what love and tears and joy go into a "simple book."

To Mike, who supports all my creative endeavors; you, my Best Beloved, are the most outstanding husband a woman could ask for, and then some! To my son and daughter, who are the best, too. I love you.

To those who encouraged me as a writer before I even knew I was one. Thank you. Thanks for planting seeds and watering them. People like you make all the difference in this world.

My beta readers and a few encouragers that deserve special mention: Miranda, Sarah, Molly, Alek, Roxandra, Adrienne, Lynne, Stef, Eileen, Eric and Errik, and especially Gemi, who paved the way and made publishing seem not a distant dream, but an achievable goal.

And to my 'project team': cover artist, Adrienne, and editors, Kelcey and Leanne, for your expertise, encouragement, and sisterhood. I'm so glad that God brought us together for this.

Author's Note

Dear Reader,

I hope you enjoyed getting to know Jenny and Andrew as much as I did; their short story turned into a novel, which turned into a trilogy, which turned into...well, you get the idea. More stories are on the way. Robert and Ryan deserve their own happy-ever-after, too, don't you think?

I'm grateful for poets and loved digging through my anthologies looking for the perfect poetry for Jenny to read. If you want to explore more works by these authors, here is a convenient list.

- *Jenny Kissed Me,* Leigh Hunt (1784-1859)
- *My True-Love Hath My Heart,* Sir Phillip Sidney (1554-1586)
- *If You But Knew,* Anonymous
- *Sally in Our Alley* (mentioned, not quoted), Henry Carey (1687-1743)

Happy reading!
April

41552067R00189

Made in the USA
Charleston, SC
02 May 2015